THE CONSTANT HEART

The Constant Heart

by
Patricia Robins

Dales Large Print Books
Long Preston, North Yorkshire,
England.

British Library Cataloguing in Publication Data.

Robins, Patricia
  The constant heart.

  A catalogue record for this book is
  available from the British Library

  ISBN 1-85389-630-6 pbk

First published in Great Britain by Hurst & Blackett Ltd.,
an imprint of the Hutchinson Group 1964

Dales Large Print is an imprint of
Library Magna Books Ltd.
Printed and bound in Great Britain by
T.J. Press (Padstow) Ltd., Cornwall, PL28 8RW.

1431232 8

1

Lower Beeches lay sleeping in the afternoon sunshine as Tamily made her way up the flagged path and through the white gate on to the rough lane which wound past the church to Allenton Manor. As she reached Ten Acre Paddock she stopped and looked back at her home with curious intensity.

The farmhouse was only just visible through the dark green yews in the churchyard; it was a dull red, the red tiled roof and the old bricks merging together to give the soft mellowness of antiquity. She loved the house. Even now she could never quite believe that it was her own.

She shivered as a sudden breeze blew up from the stream, ruffling her brown hair. She pulled the white cardigan closer round her shoulders and her mouth tightened with momentary unhappiness. It was wrong to feel cold on this hot August afternoon; wrong to feel unhappy when she had so much for which to be grateful.

Tamily began to walk on slowly, her feet in the white toeless sandals scuffing up the dust. She ought to hurry, but somehow she was not looking forward to the usual Wednesday tea with Jess. She was afraid her mother would see in her eyes that something was wrong; see and ask questions Tamily couldn't answer...

Her mind swung back through the years, remembering how as a little girl she had first come to live at the Manor when her mother took a job as housekeeper to Lord and Lady Allenton.

Dick Allenton and his sister Mercia had been young children then. Those childhood years, spent in this beautiful place, had been the happiest Tamily had ever known. Sadness had not been part of her life until she began to grow up and had fallen in love with Dick...

'Dick! Dick!' she thought. 'Our marriage was going to be so perfect...so wonderful. I was so happy...'

But first there had been the unhappy years when Dick had been at Oxford. Dick had been so young, and she, his childhood companion, could hardly have expected him to see her as a woman deeply in love with him. In fact, she had gone to impossible lengths to keep him from guessing. All the same, it hurt somewhere deep down inside that she had never loved anyone else but him and he had fallen in love three times, with Sylvia, Dorice and Anthea.

Deliberately she cut off the memory. It was the future she must guard against, not the past. The past included poor Mercia's death...Mercia whom they all still missed and whose grave was always beautifully tended and bedecked with flowers. Once a week Tamily came to the graveyard to renew the flowers, bringing Mercia's little daughter, now three, with her. They had named the baby after her mother and little Mercia was now hers and Dick's adopted child. She called them Mummy and Daddy, but Tamily used to talk to her about her mother, calling her 'Your first mummy', so that the child should not forget. No one wished to forget Mercia, who had been all goodness, all sweetness, and whose death had been an unforgettable tragedy for them all.

Yet somehow, even in her death, Mercia had brought happiness to them. It was her death which had brought Dick to Tamily's side, to the awareness at long last that he loved her. And it had given them the baby they both loved now as much as they would their own.

'I've been so lucky!' Tamily thought as she began to hurry towards the drive up to Allenton Manor. Dick's father had given them Lower Beeches and fifty acres of farmland for a wedding present and his mother had given them enough money to have the old farmhouse beautifully restored. Tamily's mother had insisted upon paying for her only daughter's wedding in the old family church on the estate and it was as lavish as Mercia's had been when she married Keith.

The only thing they had lacked was capital for Dick to start farming. How angry and resentful he had been! It had taken all Tamily's tact to make him see that his father had already been more than generous and to expect more was quite unfair.

Dick's face had been flushed and angry as he retorted:

'Father wouldn't even miss the money, Tammy. It's because he's still hoping I'll go in for politics; it's his kind of blackmail. I'm forced to get a job now whether I want it or not.'

10

Tammy understood his disappointment. He had finished his term at Oxford and got the first in history his father had wanted. Now, to have the farm, the land and no money to start it, was almost worse than having nothing. He was so near to achieving his dream, she understood his frustration.

But Lord Allenton had his reasons and Tamily could see his point of view even if Dick refused to do so. The old man had said:

'Dick's always had everything drop into his lap, Tamily. It's not good for him to have life so easy. He's spoilt and that's the truth of the matter. Now he has you—a young wife he's really done nothing at all to deserve—and it is high time he grew up. One day everything I have will be Dick's. Before I die I want to be sure that he is responsible enough to take over from me.'

In a way Dick's father was right, although his methods might seem a bit harsh. Dick *was* spoilt. It was so hard not to spoil him; not just hard for her, who loved him so much—but for his mother, for Jess, his friends; everyone loved him. He was good-looking, charming, gay, full of fun and as good with his brain as he was with his hands. The gods had been kind when they had fashioned Dick, and now, for the first time in his life, he was denied something he badly wanted.

'Let him make his own money, Tamily!' Lord Allenton had said quietly. 'He's very young—he has time on his side. Once he has made enough, he can chuck up his job and start farming if he wishes.'

'And so, by God, I will!' Dick had said furiously. 'I'll show him he can't dictate to me. He's treating me as if I were a kid!'

Tears came suddenly into Tamily's eyes, blurring her vision of the beautiful old manor house which she was now approaching. Although she was far too loyal to admit the truth even to her own mother, she knew now, after three years of marriage, that Lord Allenton was right. Dick was still a child. Somehow he was like a kind of Peter Pan. He wouldn't—or couldn't—grow up!

She brushed her hand quickly across her eyes, and as she did so she saw her mother walking towards her. Watching her as she approached, Tamily was suddenly aware of her mother's stooped back and ageing appearance.

'She's getting old!' she thought with dismay. Quickly she forced a smile to her mouth. Whatever happened, Jess must not find out that her marriage to Dick was anything but blissful.

Jess's life had been one of complete self-sacrifice, devoted to making her daughter happy. She had asked nothing more and, in return for their acceptance of Tamily as one of their own family, she had given a life-time of devoted service to Lord and Lady Allenton. Although she was still officially their housekeeper, she was now in a very privileged position where she was acting more as companion to Lady Allenton. There was a cook and two other servants who did most of the work inside the house. Jess's life was comparatively easy and very comfortable now. She was free any afternoon to come down to Tamily's house and have tea with her and baby Mercia, whom she adored.

'Darling, you're late! Nothing wrong at home?' the older woman asked as she bent and kissed Tamily's cheek.

'No, of course not! I think I was just being lazy and forgot the time!' Tamily said quickly. She linked her arm in her

13

mother's and they walked together towards the house.

'Mercia's all right?'

'Fine! She's spending the afternoon with the Jeffries. She and little Robin get on so well and she loves going to tea there.'

They walked round the side of the house to the terrace overlooking the rose garden. Tea was laid out waiting for them. Tamily sat down in one of the comfortable lounge chairs and her mother poured out the tea.

'Mercia is so like her mother!' Jess said. 'Every time I see her she seems to grow more and more like her; same soft hair and blue eyes; same delicate features; although, of course, little Mercia is as strong as a horse.'

'Wiry! That's what Dr Parker calls her!' Tamily said smiling. 'But she is like Mercia to look at, I agree. I think that's why Dick loves her so much. He dotes on the child and spoils her terribly. I have to be pretty firm with her and it isn't always easy when Dick lets her get away with murder.'

'He ought not to do that,' Jess said thoughtfully. 'A three-year-old isn't able to understand two sets of rules. You ought to have a word with Dick about it—tell him

14

he must back you up over the rules you lay down for the child.'

Tamily nodded, taking the cup of tea from her mother's hands and sipping it thoughtfully. She wasn't going to admit that there had already been words—several angry scenes, to be precise—over young Mercia. Dick refused to appreciate the need for any kind of discipline.

'After all, Tammy, she's only three! Great Scott, if a father can't spoil his daughter when she's not much bigger than a grasshopper when can he spoil her?'

'Never, if you want to do what's best for her!' Tammy had said quietly. 'Don't you see, Dick, that she has got to learn the rules: bedtime at six and saying "Please" and "Thank you"—she's got to learn that kind of thing just the same way we had to.'

But Dick refused to see her point of view—or else chose to ignore it. It was easy to see why—the tiny fair-haired child was highly intelligent and she knew only too well that she could twist Dick round her little finger. Whatever command Tamily gave her which she did not like she would reply:

'Daddy let me! I want Daddy.'

15

It wasn't fair—to her or to Mercia.

Tammy tried to curb her own impatience. She made herself remember that Dick had always blamed himself for his sister's death, although no one else blamed him. Because he had taken the family chauffeur away from the premises when Mercia's baby had been about to arrive, her husband, Keith, had had to go for the nurse. It was not Dick's fault the roads had been wet, not his fault the car had skidded and Keith had been killed. Yet he had always blamed himself, knowing, as they all did, that Mercia had not wanted to recover after the birth of her baby, preferring to join Keith whom she'd loved so much. Mercia had *wanted* to die and only Dick insisted that it was all his fault. Not that he ever spoke of it now; maybe he'd forgotten, buried the feeling of guilt somewhere in his subconscious. But Tammy felt sure this was the reason he could not bring himself to deny anything to the baby girl who looked so like his sister.

'How's Dick? I haven't seen him for nearly two weeks.'

Tamily's face was bent over her tea-cup.

16

'He's fine! He was down last weekend but there wasn't much time to come over here. You see, he couldn't get away until after lunch Saturday and he had to be back at the flat Sunday night.'

'I expect you miss him!'

'Well, in a way, of course! But I'm getting used to it!' Tamily lied hurriedly. As if she would ever get used to being separated from him, even for five days. If it weren't for Mercia she would have gone up to London with him, much as she hated the idea of living in Town.

'He seems to be doing very well. Lord Allenton was telling me the senior partner thinks very highly of him. And he's only twenty-five. It's amazing. I never thought Dick had it in him to make a successful stockbroker—of all things!'

But Tamily was not surprised at Dick's success. She knew the force of angry determination which urged him to work like a black at a job he had never wanted. She knew, none better, how easily he could charm people, lead them, persuade them; laugh away their fears or disagreements. Whatever field he had decided to take up, Dick would succeed. Failure was a word unknown to him.

Yet their marriage was beginning to fail...

'No!' She spoke the thought aloud and her mother looked at her in surprise.

'No? No what?'

Tamily bit her lip. She put her empty tea-cup back on the table and said lightly:

'I just meant that Dick and stockbroking don't seem to go together. He's always wanted to be a farmer.'

Jess looked at her daughter with dawning unease. There was something restrained about Tamily; something she could not put a name to but which she sensed was different. Not that Tamily was ever a noisy, extroverted child. But during the first year or so of her marriage to Dick she had had a glowing radiance and was so obviously rapturously happy. Now she was suddenly too quiet and there was no laughter in her eyes.

'Tam, darling, you would tell me if there was something wrong? Are you missing Dick very much? If that's it why don't you go and live in the flat with him? You know I'd have Mercia here during the week and she could be with you weekends. She'd be perfectly happy with me.'

Tamily shifted in her chair, keeping her

18

face averted from her mother's eyes.

Yes, Mercia would be happy enough. Lord and Lady Allenton adored their little grand-daughter and Jess had always been wonderful with children. But Dick had been dead set against the idea.

For the first eighteen months of their marriage he had travelled up and down to London every day. No matter how late at night, he had always come home. However long the day for her, there were always the nights in their big four-poster bed to look forward to. But as Dick had become caught up in his work he'd found the daily commuting more and more trying. Once or twice he spoke of getting a flat in Town, but they simply could not afford it and Dick was certainly not going to ask his father for money. Then he had been offered a flat by a friend and had jumped at the chance.

There were times when sheer tiredness made him irritable and she had needed all her tact and patience and love to keep from having headlong arguments with him. Dick would always 'win' any arguments they had because in the end Tamily gave way. She preferred to give in than maintain her own point of view at the too heavy price of being alienated from him. She couldn't bear Dick's anger. She couldn't bear the nights when he would lie on his side of the bed, refusing to talk to her; to kiss her good night. Inevitably she would lean closer to him, searching for his hand, saying gently:

'I'm sorry, darling. Don't let's quarrel about it. I don't really mind if that's what you want.'

Once he had turned and said:

'Well, for God's sake, you should mind. You haven't any spirit, Tam; no backbone. You're weak!'

She had been dreadfully hurt, even though she knew his accusation was only part true. She was weak where his love for her was in jeopardy. Love would always come first. She would give up anything to keep Dick's love and be glad to do so. This was something she couldn't explain to him in words and which he couldn't understand.

Mostly he accepted her surrender with a quick change of mood.

'There's my girl!' he'd say, pulling her into his arms and kissing her with quick, ready passion. His physical need of her was never far from the surface and Tamily

20

gloried in the perfection of their love-making. In this at least Dick was all hers. Even now, after nearly three years of marriage, Dick wanted her as much as he had in the first weeks of their honeymoon. But now it had begun to seem as if it were *only* in bed that they could agree.

Tamily hated the flat; hated the colleague who had first offered it to Dick for a nominal rent as he, himself, was going abroad for a year. Dick had not told Tamily about it until it was all fixed. Then he had announced his plans casually.

'It's just the job, Tam. Bedroom, kitchen and bathroom and a minute sitting-room, and all for a quid a week. Thank God for no more 8.15. I think I'd have gone mad if I'd had to catch that blasted train many more mornings.'

'But, Dick, if there's only one room where will Mercia sleep? You'll want the sitting-room for your work and...'

Dick was staring at her in frowning surprise.

'It's not a *family* flat, Tam. It's not much bigger than a large box, in fact. You and Mercia can stay on here and I'll come down weekends.'

Even Dick could not fail to notice the

21

look on her face. He had put an arm round her and hugged her.

'It'll only be four nights a week, Tam. I can go up on the 8.15 Monday mornings and I'll be down again Friday night. Really, darling, it'll be far easier all round. Don't look so miserable.'

For one of the few times in her life she had openly expressed her need of him.

'But, Dick, I don't want to live apart from you all week. I don't want to stay here alone with Mercia. I want to be with you.'

Dick patted her arm.

'Now don't be silly, Tam. You know very well we hardly see each other in the week, anyway, with me getting home so late. As to you being alone, why, there's Jess just up the road and Mother and Father and all our friends.'

But she wanted to be with him and it had hurt her beyond measure that he had not wanted it equally.

'You know London wouldn't suit Mercia. We've got to think of her. Besides, darling, you'd hate leaving Lower Beeches. You know you would.'

Yes, she would have hated leaving her home. She loved the old farmhouse and spent hours cleaning and polishing until the place shone with the loving care she gave it. But she would have willingly exchanged it to be near Dick...and her mother would, as she had just said, have looked after Mercia.

For the first month Dick had come home Friday nights and caught the 8.15 back on Monday morning. The days and nights in between had been bearable. But then, as he was caught up in his work and attendant social gatherings, it had been lunchtime Saturday and a departure Sunday evening, leaving her only one whole day of his company.

Tamily tried not to complain; he was throwing himself into his work not just for his own but for both their sakes. If he made a success of this career it would mean he could start up the farm all the sooner and then he would never have to be away from her again. She told herself this over and over again, but it was not always as easy to remember, especially when Dick showed signs of enjoying the career he had taken up so unwillingly. He would tell her what he had been doing, parties he'd been to, people he had met with a bright, glowing interest that somehow left her, his wife, out in the cold.

He never suggested she should join him even for an occasional evening, and Tamily was too proud to ask. Only once, when she had gone up to London for a day's shopping, she had asked Dick if he could take her out to lunch. He'd promised to do so, but when she'd called at the office he'd been full of apologies because Foster, the senior partner, was taking him to lunch with an important client and he had not liked to refuse.

Tamily tried to understand. She'd lunched alone at Lyons Corner House and talked herself into believing that *she* would have put Dick off at the last minute if *her* career had been at stake. But the truth of the matter was that Dick would always come first; he always had and he always would.

Tamily was intelligent enough to realize that it might be wiser to hide this complete devotion from her young husband. She knew that it sometimes irritated him because she never disagreed with him; never complained when he was short-tempered or forgetful. With a wry smile she recalled the occasion when he had forgotten her birthday, remembering it only at the

24

week-end when he'd noticed the beautiful Queen Anne tallboy his father and mother had given her as a present.

'For heaven's sake, Tammy; why didn't you remind me?'

'I didn't mind, darling!' But, of course, she *had* been terribly hurt and Dick had known it.

'I'd feel a lot better if you tore a few strips off!' Dick said flatly. 'You're too long-suffering, Tam. I don't know how you put up with me.'

'I love you!' she had told him softly. But instead of kissing her Dick had turned away and replied:

'Sometimes I wonder if you don't love me too much Tam. It isn't good to be so dependent on someone else... It...it puts a kind of special responsibility on me which I don't think I can cope with. And now I've hurt you...'

Tamily turned suddenly to her mother and said:

'*Is* it possible to love someone too much, Mother?'

Jess looked surprised.

'I shouldn't think so...not if you are talking about real love. I think people who are very much in love can be too

25

possessive, too demanding. But if you're thinking of yourself, my dear, I don't think there's much you can do to change your nature. It's always been that way between you and Dick, hasn't it? Ever since you were children.'

'Yes, always!' Tamily said.

Jess watched her daughter's hands twisting restlessly in her lap with increasing unease. Something was wrong. Young Dick away too much? Was he beginning to take his wife for granted?

Jess was very fond of Dick. She had known him since he was a boy in short trousers, and she was well aware of his faults as well as his virtues. But there was no real badness in him, only a thoughtlessness which had got him into scrapes as a child and which might now be causing difficulties in his marriage.

'Dick not only loves you very much, Tamily, but he needs you, too. His temperament is like quicksilver and your calm dependable type of nature is just what he needs to anchor him.'

Tamily nodded. Privately she thought: 'All the same, I sometimes wonder if Dick wants an anchor!'

But she put the thought away. Theirs

26

was a wonderful marriage. Each knew the other so well there had been no difficult beginning period when they had had to discover each other as people. There had been only the joy of discovering their physical delight in one another and that had been completely perfect and satisfying to them both. It still was. Tamily never felt so completely sure of Dick's love as she did in moments of love-making. Then he was all hers—body and soul, as the old song said.

'You are quite a different person when you make love, Tam!' he'd once told her. 'It's almost as if you were asleep at other times; you're so quiet and restrained and controlled. But like this'...he had touched her naked body with a kind of awe...'like this you are on fire and it sets me alight, too.'

Maybe she was too passive, too quiet, as a rule. But it wasn't in her to be extroverted. The things she felt most deeply she hid inside herself. It was only with the act of love that she could really express all she felt; as if Dick freed her from that restraint he had tried to describe.

Tamily sighed and stretched her arms above her head. How stupid she was to feel so depressed when she had so much to be grateful for. Only three short years ago she had not even dared to hope that Dick might one day grow to love her. Now he was her husband; she had a beautiful home which one day Dick would live in all the time. They had Mercia, and once Dick had a bit of money behind him there would be children of their own, too. They had fifty acres of good land which was being cared for by Lord Allenton's bailiff, Adam Bond. Under his management the land was prospering, and when Dick took over he would be off to a fine start.

And not only all this, but she lived near to her own much-loved mother and to her mother-in-law and father-in-law, who treated her with as much loving kindness as they had shown their daughter Mercia. Indeed, Lord Allenton was much nicer to her than to Dick, whom he persisted in calling 'a spoiled young puppy'. But for Tamily, he said, he'd have turfed Dick out on his ear to rough it a bit after he'd finished at Oxford. But for all his apparent toughness with his son, Tamily knew the old man loved Dick dearly and wanted only what he thought would be good for him. Tamily could see both points of view.

Dick had been born with a silver spoon in his mouth and in a way he was a little spoiled. But, equally, she could understand Dick's resentment at being kept short of money when there was no need. Lord Allenton could certainly have afforded to lend them capital to start the farm. One day all his money would go to Dick, so why not now, when they both wanted to be together and fulfil Dick's childhood dream? Lord Allenton was not a snob—he had no objection to Dick farming. It was simply that he intended to make him 'stand on his own feet', as he put it; and learn how 'the other half lived'.

Tamily dropped a kiss on her mother's grey head.

'I'm just going to look in on Father!' she said. 'He'll have had his nap now. I'll come out and say goodbye before I go home.'

Jess watched her daughter's slim young figure disappear through the french windows into the drawing-room. Her moment of worry passed. Tamily was not unhappy—and that was the only care she had in the world.

Lord Allenton was sitting at his desk in the study as Tamily entered. He looked with pleasure at his daughter-in-law. He was very, very fond of Tamily. She was a sensible, straight-forward, thoroughly nice girl and Dick was a lucky young devil to have such a wife. Pretty, too. She looked charming in a flowered cotton frock leaving her arms bare and darkly tanned by the sun. Strange to think that the little tomboy who had shinned up trees with Dick had blossomed into this rounded, lovely young woman.

She bent and kissed his cheek, her lips soft and warm against his dried-up old skin.

'How nice you look, my dear. How are you?'

'I'm fine, Father. Mercia sent you a kiss. She's playing with little Robin Jeffries this afternoon, but I'm bringing her to tea here tomorrow.'

Lord Allenton nodded.

'Sit down, Tamily. I'm rather glad to have the chance of a few minutes alone. Fact is, my dear, I'm a bit worried about Bond. He's out of hospital and came to see me this morning to report back for work. Frankly, I didn't much like the look of him. I'm not at all sure he ought to be working yet, but he swears he's all right.'

Tamily raised her eyebrows.

'I didn't know he was ill. I thought he'd gone into hospital for an eye operation.'

'So he did. But he looks—well, I don't quite know how to describe it—beaten.'

'Would you like me to call in on my way home and see him?' Tamily offered.

Lord Allenton smiled.

'I hoped you'd suggest that. Of course, there may be nothing wrong, but I'd like to be sure. Good chap, Bond. I wasn't too sure about him when I took him on after old Matthews retired, but he's more than proved his worth.'

'Dick likes him, too,' Tamily agreed. 'Don't worry, I'll drop in and see him. It's a pity there's no wife to take care of him.'

She left her father-in-law a few minutes later and after saying goodbye to her mother she went down the drive to the Lodge, where once Mercia and Keith had lived and which the bailiff now occupied. She, too, liked Adam Bond. He was of a generation between her own and Dick's and his parents; a man who couldn't be far off forty and looked it, yet was, so Dick had once told her, not quite thirty-five. He was a little under six foot, dark-haired, broad-shouldered. He had rather beautiful,

31

unusual hazel eyes which seldom smiled, although he was a man with a sense of humour. He had a wonderful way with animals—possessing that particular quiet firm kind of voice which animals and children, judging by young Mercia, understood and respected.

Respect was the operative word, Tamily decided. One did respect Adam. He worked with untiring energy on the Allenton estate and without any apparent sudden changes had managed to completely modernize and make economical the farms of which Lower Beeches was one.

Her mother had told her some weeks ago that Adam had gone into hospital for an operation. But Tamily knew nothing beyond the fact that it had something to do with his eyes.

Bond came to the door in answer to her knock and for a moment stood looking down at her as if he wasn't quite sure who it could be. Then, pulling himself together, he said:

'Mrs Dick! How nice to see you. Won't you come in?'

She smiled back at him and followed him into the office in which he did all the estate work; he used the same room for a sitting-room, furnishing it only with a couple of deep leather armchairs and a side table for his pipe and ashtray.

'How are you, Adam?' Tamily asked as she sat down in the leather chair. She was still a little shy using his Christian name, but Dick always did and it seemed somehow unfriendly to go on using his surname; almost as if he were an inferior.

The man looked away from her and busied himself finding and lighting his pipe. He was afraid of betraying to this girl what the mere sight of her had done to him. The sight of anything beautiful now had the power to unnerve him completely, leaving him trembling and almost as if physically afraid.

He had known for a week now that within a year he would be blind. He wondered if others facing a similar fate were affected in the same way by the loveliness of life which would soon be denied to them.

'I'm well enough,' he said quickly.

'Lord Allenton asked me to drop by and see you. He was a little worried about you,' Tamily said.

A faint smile passed across the man's face, softening it. 'That was kind of him.

And kind of you, Mrs Dick.'

Tamily said shyly:

'I wish you'd call me Tamily—everyone else does. Was it grim in hospital?'

Adam perched himself on the office chair and puffed meditatively at his pipe. He shook his head.

'Not too bad. Though, being an outdoor type, I hated being cooped in, especially when I wasn't really ill. It's good to be out—to see the flowers and trees and the corn in the fields!'

'Like seeing them all for the first time!'

Tamily was quite unprepared for the quick, searching look of surprise the man gave her. Or for his words as he said:

'How did you guess?'

Tamily smiled.

'I don't know. Tell me, the operation was a success, wasn't it? You're quite all right now?'

Adam Bond walked over to the window and stared into the massive chestnut trees which lined the drive outside the Lodge. For the first time in his life he was desperately lonely for someone near and dear to him. His whole family had been wiped out in the Blitz and he had been brought up with elderly foster-parents in the country to where he had been evacuated. Now they, too, were dead and he had no one in the world to whom he belonged; in whom he could confide.

Until recently when he had first felt an aching pain behind his eyes he had not been conscious of his solitariness. He had been perfectly content working on the Allenton estate. He was by nature self-sufficient, and in any event there was little time to be lonely. Occasionally he would go down to the pub to join some of the estate workers in a drink, but more often he would sit in the garden in summer, or over the fire smoking his pipe and reading. Once or twice he had been invited to dinner with Dick and Tamily, but not for some time now, as Dick spent so much of his time in London.

Adam was fond of the young couple. There was no 'side' about Dick, although one day he would be Lord Allenton and own this whole place. Dick had done Oxford the easy way; Adam had worked the hard way through grammar school to agricultural college.

Adam thought Tamily one of the most delightful young women he had ever met. She reminded him of a girl he had once loved, a student at the college, whose features were so like Tamily's that it had shaken him a bit the first time Dick had introduced her to him. But Tamily was far sweeter, more gentle and charming than Bunty, who had tortured him with uncertainty, full of promises she never meant to keep and finally leaving him for a New Zealander.

But that was an old story and he'd never fallen in love again. And now there was no one left to whom he could tell the frightening news the eye specialist had given him; that the operation had merely postponed the inevitable. Within a year at the latest he would be quite blind.

Quite suddenly he heard himself telling Tamily the facts. He spoke jerkily, slowly, as if the confidence were painful. In a way he was listening to himself saying aloud what, until now, he had refused to face.

'It will mean giving up my job, of course. I shall have to tell Lord Allenton soon and give him time to find a replacement.

Tamily's face was white with shock. Adam Bond was almost a stranger; he played no part in her life other than as an occasional guest in her home; someone whom Dick liked and respected and who would ultimately be his guide and adviser when he took over the farm himself. But, always highly sensitive, Tamily felt the full impact of the man's fear and loneliness. All that was capable of pity and sympathy rose up in her so that she was on her feet, her hand on Adam's arm as she said:

'Oh, Adam! I'm so sorry. How awful for you!'

He was touched by her concern. She really looked distressed and in a strange way that was comforting. Of course, the nurses in the hospital had known the trouble and pitied him, but their pity was impersonal. Somehow Tamily's was not.

'I expect I'll get used to it in time. At the moment all I can do is stare at everything as if I were seeing the beauty of the world around me for the first time. Those were your words, I think!' He smiled at her wryly. 'It's strange that one doesn't realize how much beauty there is until one is about to lose sight of it for ever.'

'Can't anything be done?' Tamily asked angrily. 'Surely these days, there is some-thing—?'

'No, nothing!' he interrupted quietly. 'It's due to a severe head injury I had as a child in the Blitz. That was when

I lost my family. I'm lucky that I've had all these years. The specialist said it could have happened at any time.'

'But what will you do?' Tamily asked.

'Go to St Dunstan's. At least with the Welfare State I shall be well looked after. In time I'll learn some other trade which the blind can do and earn my living that way.'

'But no more farming!' Tamily cried. 'You'll *hate* that!'

'Yes! I try not to think about it. I've lots to be thankful for, you know. Thirty-five years of sight, for one. And then I've no responsibilities, no wife and children dependent on me. It could all be much worse.'

Tamily swallowed and moved away from him.

'You're very brave.'

'Not really. Inside I'm pretty much of a coward. I ought not to have bothered you with my troubles, anyway. It was just that...well, I think it must have been that remark of yours about seeing things for the first time. Incidentally, I'd be grateful if you'd keep the fact to yourself. I don't want the men guessing—at least, not until nearer the time. It'll happen suddenly, you see—no gradual loss of sight. One morning I'll wake up and it'll be dark—so the specialist says. I might begin to get the pain back a week or two beforehand, but that will stop once I am blind. Please don't think about it anymore. You looked so young and carefree when you came in just now...I'd hate to think I was responsible for that worried line on your forehead.'

Tamily attempted a smile, but it was very self-conscious. She knew he was staring at her, but realized, also, that he would stare at everything now, soaking up the outline and colour and shape of things like a thirsty man soaks up water he knows will soon no longer be available.

She said:

'Dick will be so upset, too.'

'Don't tell him,' Adam said quietly. 'Not yet, anyway. It may sound silly, but I'd like everything to go on as usual as long as it possibly can.'

Tamily nodded.

'I'll keep the secret, but on one condition. You'll come to dinner with us on Saturday. Dick has promised to get home early and only last weekend he said it was a long time since he had had a good long "jaw" with you.'

'Thanks, I'd enjoy that,' the man told her as they walked towards the door.

He stood in the doorway, watching Tamily's departing figure as she disappeared up the tree-lined drive. How young she looked! How fresh and attractive in the flowered frock, her arms and legs bare and golden-brown from the sun.

He turned back indoors with a sigh. There was never any happiness to be had from envying others, he told himself sharply. Yet at that moment he was filled with envy of young Dick Allenton. Not only had he a family, home and a lovely young wife, but eyes with which he would continue to see the magnificence of his surroundings.

2

Dick lay on the thickly carpeted floor of the drawing-room of his flat, the telephone tucked under his chin while with his free hands he lit a cigarette. His face was puckish with laughter.

'No, I can't possibly, Carol. I've got work to do!'

Across the wires the girl's American accent was even more marked than when he'd spoken to her during lunch yesterday.

'But, honey, you've gotta eat. I promise I won't keep you out late.'

Dick's voice was full of regret.

'I'd love to, Carol, but really I have got a pile of work to do, and, anyway, I've already eaten.'

'But, honey, it's only eight o'clock!'

Dick laughed.

'I know. I bought something at the delicatessen on the way back from the office and I've just finished eating it. I'm having coffee right now.'

'Then let me join you for coffee!'

Dick felt a mixture of exasperation and pleasure. Carol Holmer was an extremely attractive girl of nineteen. Not only was she beautiful, she was also very rich. He'd met her for the first time yesterday, when he'd lunched with the firm's latest client, Harry D. Holmer, and had been both delighted and surprised when the American had brought his only daughter with him.

It *was* flattering to have a young girl fall in a heap at your feet in twenty-four hours flat. Carol had flirted with him all through lunch, casting him meaningful glances through the long silky loop of fair hair which hung down over one side of the perfect oval of her face. It hadn't needed any intelligence to get the message from those incredibly long slanting green eyes that sparkled even more than the champagne they were drinking.

All the same, Dick was English enough to expect a woman to let the man make the running. And this was the second time Carol had telephoned him today; once this morning at the office to say how much she'd enjoyed yesterday's lunch. Possibly she'd been hoping then he'd invite her to lunch again! Now this evening...

'Look, Carol, this is a bachelor establishment. It's not a suitable place for entertaining lovely young females. I'd love to see you, but—'

'I don't care what kind of rat-trap you live in, honey. Give me the address and I'll be right over—just so long as you really do want to see me.'

Her voice dropped on the last words, becoming husky and, Dick told himself, distinctly sexy.

He hesitated a moment longer. This was Friday and he'd promised Tammy he'd do his damnedest to get away early tomorrow; try to make a long weekend of it. If he let Carol come over now it meant working until the early hours or else catching a train down to the country after rather than before lunch.

He sighed. Poor old Tam—it really was a bit lonely for her stuck down there all week with only young Mercia for company. And she did try so hard not to complain. But the look in her eyes on Sunday nights was enough to make him feel thoroughly guilty, wondering whether he ought not to stay and make the effort to get up early and catch that blasted 8.15 Monday morning instead.

Then he shrugged his shoulders. He'd managed before on a few hours' sleep; he'd get Carol out of the place by 10.30 at the latest and then get down to work. With any luck he'd be through by midnight or soon after.

'Okay, Carol. Here's the address. But you'll have to go hungry. There's nothing but a pâte sandwich left.'

He tried to concentrate on his work while he waited for the girl to arrive. But his mind kept turning over the unexpected situation that had arisen. It was all a bit of a fluke really. Foster, the senior partner, was supposed to have lunched Mr Holmer yesterday. Then Foster's wife had been rushed off to hospital with peritonitis and he'd rung up from home to tell Dick to go to the lunch in his place.

Mr Holmer was someone important enough to be given the works. It was up to Dick to see he had everything he wanted. Nobody had mentioned he had a daughter—certainly not that she was a stunning nineteen-year-old and, since she had been in England only a few days, completely unattached.

'I'd be real grateful if you could show my baby round a bit,' Mr Holmer had said to Dick. 'This is a kinda educational tour for her and she hasn't seen London before. If you could spare the time, Mr Allenton, we'd sure appreciate it!'

Carol had looked hard into Dick's eyes and he had grinned back.

'It'll be my pleasure!' he'd said.

So this wasn't altogether being unfair to Tammy. It was business, really. Foster would be furious if Dick antagonized the Holmers and keeping Carol happy was obviously the way to keep Daddy happy, too.

Dick grinned to himself. So far he'd not found much about stockbroking to like. True enough, he'd found it exciting sometimes. True, he was making money himself. But there wasn't much light relief—not much fun for anyone like himself with a love of gaiety. But this could be fun. Dangerous, too. Better tell the girl right away he was married so she knew the score. If she still wanted him to show her London then he'd enjoy it, too. Be a welcome relief, this hot exhausting August, to get out of the office...

It was nearly an hour before Carol arrived. Obviously, she had taken time changing. Like most American girls she was meticulously neat and fresh-looking, and quite stunning in a dead white linen sheath dress which was relieved only by a long dangling gold chain hanging between the barely discernible cleft of her high breasts.

'Wow!' Dick greeted her. 'You're a sight for sore eyes!'

She smiled, taking the compliment easily.

'Thank you! I've brought some champagne—thought you might want cooling off. My, it's hot!'

Dick wore only an open-necked cotton shirt and tight blue denim jeans. He pointed to them apologetically.

'Sorry I haven't changed.'

Carol looked him up and down coolly, then stared directly into his eyes.

'You look okay to me!' she said softly.

Dick dropped his eyes. He was faintly uneasy with this girl. For all Carol was only nineteen, she was very poised, very sophisticated and completely sure of herself. He wished he felt as sure of himself. The fact was, she was more than a little exciting and now that he was a respectably married man he ought not to feel that heady attraction for anyone but Tammy.

'Look, Carol!' he said as she uncorked the champagne and found two plain glass tumblers to pour it into. 'There's something I ought to tell you right away. I think you should know that I'm married. My wife'...he paused, remembering Tammy's soft, pleading eyes...'my wife lives in the country. I go home every weekend to be with her.'

He did not see the faint flickering of the girl's long darkened eyelashes. Taking the glass from him, she took a long drink before she said:

'Tell me about her. What does she look like? Is she English? Sit down here and tell me all about her.'

She patted the divan beside her. Dick felt happier. At least now Carol knew the facts. What happened next—if anything—was up to her. All the same, he wouldn't risk sitting so close to her. He squatted down on the floor at her feet.

'Tammy,' he said slowly, 'is probably the sweetest girl in the world. She's...well, she's just Tammy. I've known her pretty well all my life. She was a kind of companion as a child to my young sister, Mercia, who was an invalid in those days. Mercia died some years ago and when Tammy and I were married we adopted Mercia's little girl who is called after her.'

'So you married your childhood sweetheart!'

Dick shook his head.

'No, not exactly. It was strange, really, but for a long while I never realized Tammy was grown up. She was more like a sister to me. I had a few affairs with other girls and it wasn't until Mercia died that I discovered it was really Tammy I wanted all along.'

As if the action were quite unconscious, Carol threaded a long red-tipped finger through one of Dick's untidy curls.

'Is she attractive?'

Dick pouted.

'Well, it's hard to describe her. Attractive, yes! But she's not the glamour-type, if that's what you mean. She has very beautiful large brown eyes. There's a vaguely Italian look about her—she has that kind of golden skin. She was incredibly skinny as a little girl, all angles and bones, but she's filled out now, although I don't think she could ever be fat. Tammy is—well, she's just Tammy and everyone loves her.'

'Including you. It's strange, but she doesn't really sound your type, Dick. I would have imagined something rather small and kittenish, I think, for you.'

Dick laughed.

'I don't think I've got a "type". I like *all* pretty women!'

'And they like you!' Carol said shrewdly. 'You're a very attractive young man, Mr Dick Allenton, if I am permitted to say so. Frankly, it surprises me a little to hear you are married. You don't strike me as the "settling-down-young" type. I thought you a typical gay young bachelor.'

Dick laughed again. He was conscious now of the girl's cool fingers at the back of his neck. Her voice was low and husky and...yes, once again it was sexy and he felt himself responding to it.

'I'm a very staid married man!' he said firmly. 'I work very hard and I'm very faithful to my wife.'

Suddenly Carol laughed. Her laughter was deep-throated and exciting. Surprised, he swung round to face her.

'What's so funny?' he asked.

'You! You don't have to go on about her, Dick. I take your point—you're married. All the same, your wife isn't here now, is she? So I don't see why we shouldn't have ourselves a good time. Daddy said to me have a good time. He liked you. He approved of you.'

Dick grimaced.

'Do you only visit strictly bachelor flats when Daddy approves of their owners?'

It was Carol's turn to smile.

'I do just what I want and let Daddy do the approving afterwards. I'm very spoilt. It's what comes of having a parent with far too much money. I was born with a golden—not even just silver—spoon in my mouth.'

Dick nodded.

'I suppose that goes for me, too. But *my* father suddenly took it into his head to withhold the necessary.'

He told her briefly about his home and how he'd come to be on the Stock Exchange.

'All I really want to do is farm!' he ended.

'Poor old Dick!' Carol said, holding out her glass for more champagne. 'Now I see why you were so insistent about your work. You aren't trying to "get on"—just to make some cash to buy what you want.'

'That's about it!' Dick said. 'I've given

myself a maximum of five years in which to save enough to make a start. Five years wasted as far as I see it. Still, it has its compensations, I suppose.'

'Me, for example?' Carol looked up at him through her lashes as he handed her back the full glass.

Dick nodded.

'Yes, you! Though, unfortunately, pretty girls like you don't appear on my doorstep very often—in fact, never before, if you want the truth.'

'And what will you do with me now I am here?'

'Depends what you want, Carol.'

She accepted the ball back in her court and decided to let the issue rest for a while. When Dick was seated again, this time beside her, she said thoughtfully:

'Maybe you could get your money in less than five years. Maybe in six months.'

Dick shook his head.

'Not a hope!' he said.

'There might be. Daddy has a big deal brewing. I know all the signs if not the details. But I could find out. What Daddy puts his money into is always a sure thing, Dick. It isn't even a gamble. Back home they call him Dollar Dan. He makes them faster than I can spend them...and that's saying something!'

'It's nice of you, Carol, but, you see, I just haven't got the capital to play around with.'

Again Carol decided to let the matter ride for a while. Maybe she could arrange that, too, if there was something in it for her. And it wasn't money she wanted—it was Dick. Only she wasn't sure yet just how much she wanted him.

'You going down to the country tomorrow?' she asked.

Dick nodded.

'It'll be pretty dreary in Town without you!'

'I'll be back Monday...' Dick began, and then stopped as an idea came to him. 'Look, Carol, why don't you and your father come back with me? Maybe it would interest you to see the Manor...it's very beautiful, you know, and very old. Mother and Father would be delighted to meet you—Tammy, too. What about it, Carol?'

He didn't add that he was sure Foster would cough up for the expenses under the heading of entertainment. Foster might be a bit sticky at times, but at least he wasn't mean when it came to treating clients. It'd be fun, too, taking Carol around. Americans always loved tradition and Allenton was practically feudal still.

'We'd just love it!' Carol said warmly. 'You're quite sure your wife won't mind?'

Dick shook his head.

'Tammy'll love to meet you,' he said, warming to the idea. That was one of the wonderful things about Tam—she never objected to anything he wanted. A gay house party would be fun for her, too. He'd phone her tomorrow—give her time to get Jess down to help with the food. They could dine Saturday night at the Manor and have Sunday lunch at home, or the other way round.

'That's fixed, then,' he said. 'We'll catch the 12.15.'

'I guess Daddy will prefer to hire a car so we can see a bit of the countryside,' said Carol. 'He hates trains, and I do, too. They're always so dirty.'

Dick looked at her immaculate white dress, trying to imagine Carol in the weekend rush hour at the gloomy station. No, she didn't belong in trains. Then, as his eyes travelled upwards to her smooth porcelain white neck and face, his eyes met hers and there was no mistaking the expression in them. She looked like a soft, white cat sitting patiently watching from those slanting green eyes—watching and waiting...

'Carol, I...'

His arms went out to touch her, then to hold her and the next moment he was kissing her with a wild intoxication that was partly evoked by her, partly by the champagne.

'My God, Carol, you're so lovely, so cool and lovely!'

But she wasn't cool any longer. The bare skin of her arms burned beneath his hands. He felt his own body damp with sweat beneath his shirt. Then her hands reached inside his shirt and he felt her long sharp nails digging into his back.

Just for a moment he remembered the soft, sweet warmth of Tammy; of her voice whispering to him in the darkness:

'I could never let anyone but you make love to me, Dick.'

And his own muffled reply:

'No one but you, my darling!'

But now, suddenly, Tammy, the past and the future were forgotten. The young

American girl was all he could think of; all he wanted. He hadn't meant this to happen—hadn't wanted it to happen. But Carol did...and he was not proof against the temptation. The champagne, the heat, their proximity, Carol's strange exotic perfume...all were mingling in his senses, destroying thought and leaving only a swift burning desire in its wake.

It was all over very quickly. Dick turned away from the girl, strangely uneasy. There was none of the warm lethargic peace that followed love-making with Tam; only a nasty niggling feeling of guilt and remorse at having cheated her; and a faint distaste for the hungry grasping passion of the girl beside him.

How strangely at variance with their appearances girls were, Dick thought, as he reached for a cigarette and drew in the nicotine hurriedly. Carol had looked so cool, so distant and restrained, and yet she had been fiercely demanding, almost feline in her single-minded purpose. Tammy, when he thought about it, had a warm Italian beauty which promised a fierce possessive passion yet which, in fact, concealed a deep gentle love that was all giving.

He stood up quickly, pulling on his clothing, and said:

'I'm going to have a bath, Carol. It's so hot!'

He did not look at her but hurried into the tiny bathroom where he lay in lukewarm water, soaking. The fact was, he thought wryly, he felt unclean, not just physically either. He had satisfied an entirely momentary, meaningless physical appetite at the expense of his marriage. Not that Tammy need ever know. She would never know, he'd see to that. All the same, he would have it on his conscience that he'd been unfaithful to her.

He rubbed himself dry and went through into his bedroom to find a clean shirt and trousers. When he returned Carol was still lying across the divan, relaxed, sleepy-looking and smiling.

'You're quite a guy, Dick. I guess I'm a little in love with you.'

He stood staring down at her, awkwardly, feeling that he should at least kiss her. But he had no desire to do so. He lit another cigarette and said as gently as possible:

'I'm really what I think you would call a "heel". I am married, Carol, and I love my wife.'

Carol pouted. She did not look particularly upset. It was almost as if she had not taken his remark seriously. She said:

'Sure! Don't let it get you down, honey. I'm not.'

Dick turned away and said:

'I expect you'd like a bath. I'll run one for you.'

While she was bathing, he sat at his desk, fingering his papers. He wished desperately now that he hadn't invited Carol and her father down to Allenton. He wondered if he could somehow back out of it, but remembered irritably that he was in no position to antagonize Carol and, through her, her father. Somehow he'd have to get through the weekend. He'd better warn Carol to be careful what she said to Tammy.

Carol listened to his faltering warnings with cool unconcern.

'I'm not a complete fool, Dick. Can't you stop worrying about what's happened. I'm no innocent young virgin whom you've seduced.' She blew smoke into his face and laughed. 'I wanted you and I came here this evening to have you. I got what I wanted and I gather you had no objections?'

Dick shook his head.

'I'm sorry if I sound—well, ungrateful. The fact is, this is the first time I've been unfaithful to my wife. I—suppose I have a bit of a conscience about her—and you.'

'Well, you can rest easy over me!' Carol said sharply. 'I couldn't count the number of men I've made love with. I've no old-fashioned ideas about saving myself for the marriage bed. From what I've seen of marriages back home nothing will make them last. My mother married three times, my father twice. Most of their friends are divorced or heading that way. My own considered opinion is that the more experience you have, the better chance you have of making a marriage stick when you do finally sign on the dotted line. Not that I intend to get married for a while yet. Why should I?'

Dick was slightly shocked. He was certainly not strait-laced and he'd been around a bit himself. The old moral standards of his mother and father had gone out with the last war. All the same, his generation didn't take sex quite as casually or cynically as Carol. Girls were at least in love with the men they slept with—or thought they were. Carol's attitude seemed more that of a man; take it where you can get it. It wasn't a very nice thought. Yet he had to admit to and admire her honesty. There were no recriminations, no tears or reproaches.

'Do I scare you?' Carol asked into the silence. 'If I'm cynical I have reason to be. I'm filthy rich and yet I know money doesn't buy happiness.'

'It could certainly buy mine!' said Dick with an effort to be flippant. 'If I could start my farm and never see London again I couldn't be more happy.'

Carol came across the room and bent to kiss him lightly on the cheek.

'Maybe I'll give you a cheque for Christmas!' she said.

Dick grinned.

'Wish you could. Do you realize, Carol, I need at least eight thousand pounds. You work that out in dollars—I can't.'

Carol did some mental arithmetic.

'So!' She shrugged her shoulders. 'That's not so much. I'll ask Daddy about this deal that's coming off and let you know. Now I'm loving and leaving you, honey. I'm hungry and you want to get back to work. See you tomorrow, huh?'

Dick saw her into a taxi and went slowly

back upstairs to the flat. Carol's perfume still lingered in all the rooms, a reminder of her presence. He tried to settle down to work, but could not. It was getting on for eleven o'clock and he was suddenly tempted to ring Tammy. He reached for the phone and then put it down again. She was probably in bed asleep. It wasn't fair to wake her.

He wished he was with her. There was something safe and warm and secure about Tammy. Whatever else went on in the great big world, Tammy never changed. Then he knew that he was glad he was not with her. He had no desire to face those large, questioning brown eyes of hers. The trouble with Tammy was she was too acute; she sensed his feelings in the most uncanny way. Sometimes it was just fine...she'd know he was upset or irritable or just plain wanting her and react accordingly. Suppose she were to sense what has just happened between him and Carol?

He shrugged his shoulders.

That was absurd—as if she would—or could! All the same, it was as well he did not have to look her in the eyes tonight. And tomorrow there would be

Carol and her father until bedtime and by then he'd be at ease with Tammy and his conscience.

He gathered up the papers on his desk and stuffed them into the top drawer. They'd have to wait till Sunday evening. He couldn't stay home until Monday morning, anyway, since it would be absurd to let the Holmers drive back to Town Sunday evening without him. He'd work when he got back Sunday night.

He emptied the last of the champagne into his tooth-mug, switched off the lights and went to bed.

3

'Why must I have my lunch now? I want my lunch with Daddy. Why can't I have lunch with Daddy?'

Tamily restrained the impulse to slap the child. Mercia was being extremely trying and there was so much to be done before Dick arrived with his guests. Tamily felt faintly aggrieved that he had not given her more warning—but that was typical of Dick; he always took it for granted that everything would be all right.

She lifted some mashed potato on to a fork and put it in Mercia's mouth, temporarily silencing her. Something would have to be done with Mercia soon—she was getting quite out of hand. The main difficulty was in believing that such a tiny, elfin-like, adorable-looking child could behave so abominably! She could sit there, looking like a tiny angel even when she was in one of her tantrums.

As soon as she could, Tamily hurried Mercia upstairs for her afternoon rest and ran downstairs to the dining-room. Mercia had upset the carefully arranged bowl of roses on the table, and although Tamily had mopped up the water to save the polished surface, the flowers had still to be rearranged.

In the kitchen Sandra was cooking lunch under Tamily's direction. Fortunately, with the weather being so hot, most of the food was cold: smoked salmon to start with, followed by chicken and ham mousse—one of Jess's specialities which she had made for the main course; peaches in brandy to follow. Dick had told her to lay on a lavish meal, as the Holmers were rolling in money and used to the best of everything.

Tamily sighed. In a way she enjoyed the chance to entertain in her lovely home, but, on the other hand, she had so little time alone with Dick. Now the whole weekend would be taken up with guests and she would be lucky to have even a few minutes of Dick's company to herself.

She hoped Mercia was not going to be difficult. It would be quite like her to decide to play up just when Tamily particularly wanted her to be good. She would send her up to Jess to look after except that Dick would object. He liked to

63

have the child around as much as possible. Tamily would have approved had it not been for him spoiling her and giving in to each little whim of the child's.

As soon as the table flowers were arranged to her satisfaction, Tamily went up to her bedroom to change into a clean cotton frock. As she pulled it on over her dark curls, she looked at herself in the glass and smiled ruefully. The orange and white and green floral pattern was as much out of date as the full skirt and heart-shaped neckline. Really, she should have bought some new summer dresses, but then she usually wore jeans, or, if the weather was very hot, shorts. It seemed such a waste of money to buy clothes when Dick was trying to save every penny to start his farm, so for the most part she 'made do' with dresses she had brought for her honeymoon three years ago.

Allenton village did not sport any dress shops, and Wilstown, the nearest country town, was fifteen miles away. Once every three months or so Tamily went in to Wilstown with Jess to buy Mercia's clothes, but she usually came away without anything for herself. There was a reason for this Dick did not know, but upstairs in her bedroom wardrobe she had one hundred pounds saved up from the housekeeping and dress allowances Dick gave her. When it reached the total of two hundred pounds she was going to present it to him as her own special offering for their farm stock. It was a secret joy to think of the delighted surprise on Dick's face.

Tamily smiled, suddenly happy again because soon Dick would be here and even if they were not alone he would be close to her where she could watch his smile and listen to his gay enthusiastic voice. Dick had a wonderful facility for making everyone laugh. It would be a gay weekend, whatever the guests were like. Even the stuffiest could not hold out against Dick when he set out to charm them.

She suddenly remembered that she had invited Adam Bond for dinner. It would make odd numbers, but it did not really matter having an extra man, especially Adam. Although very quiet, he had perfect manners and was never dull, holding strong personal convictions which could draw him, shyly at first and then with growing enthusiasm, into quite exciting debates. John and Helen Jeffries, her nearest neighbours and closest friends, always had a nice word to say about Adam, liking him as much as she and Dick did. His position as Lord Allenton's bailiff did slightly complicate the social contact where mutual friends of Lord and Lady Allenton and Dick were concerned, but Dick was no snob and, because he liked Adam, apparently ignored the social distinction his father made.

Even though she was married to Dick now and would one day be Lady Allenton, Tamily could never forget that she was once just the housekeeper's daughter. She had always been treated as an equal with Mercia and Dick when they were children, but she had never felt equal or dared to consider that Dick might one day fall in love with and marry her. The Allenton's family tree went back to Norman times and the little village was so untouched by modern life that the great levelling of the classes had not really touched them or their way of life. The estate workers were well paid, well housed and happy, and the sons followed their fathers into their jobs just as they had in pre-war years. Strikes and disputes were unheard of and there wasn't a man working under Adam who wished he was in some other job elsewhere. It was almost an ideal community, with Lord Allenton, kindly and strictly fair, at their head.

Tamily's thoughts were interrupted by the sound of a car in the lane. She ran to the window and looked out to see a hired Daimler coming to a halt outside the house. With a little flush, partly nervous, partly excited, she ran downstairs to greet Dick and the visitors.

Dick came into the house first, carrying a large white pigskin suitcase. The chauffeur followed him, carrying two more smaller cases. Tamily stood, wide-eyed, watching and wondering why so much luggage was necessary for one short weekend. Then, as Dick put down his case and gave her a quick kiss on the top of her head, Carol Holmer came into the hall, followed by her father.

The first thing Tamily noticed about the other girl was her cool blonde beauty; the second, the perfectly cut pale pink linen suit which had surely been tailored to her flawless figure.

'Tam, this is Carol Holmer and her father, Mr Holmer...my wife!'

Tamily smiled shyly, but there was no

67

real answering warmth in Carol's returned gaze. She seemed to be sizing Tamily up as she stood cool and unconcerned, staring back at her.

'Sweet little unsophisticated kid!' she was thinking disparagingly. 'Quite attractive, but certainly nothing serious by way of competition for Dick's attentions. Now I wonder why he married *her?*'

Tamily led the way upstairs to the best of the two spare rooms where Carol was to sleep, while Dick followed with the cases. Mr Holmer was still downstairs giving the chauffeur instructions when to call for them on the following day.

'What a charming room!' Carol said as she looked round. There was some beautiful Queen Anne furniture in here which Lord and Lady Allention had given the young couple out of the manor house. The wide uneven floor boards shone from hundreds of years of polishing and were covered by two lovely Persian rugs. The curtains and bedspreads were a lime green unglazed chintz, which looked beautiful with the dark wood and soft warm colours of the rugs.

'The house is of the Queen Anne period,' Dick explained. 'I though you might find it interesting. When you're ready, Carol, I'll show you round the rest of the house.'

He went downstairs to take Carol's father to his smaller room on the other side of the house. Tamily offered to help Carol unpack.

'No thanks, honey—I'll manage!' Carol rejected the offer of friendship firmly. She had no intention of making friends with Dick's wife.

'Then I'll leave you and go and see how lunch is coming along!' Tamily said politely. 'That is, if there is nothing I can get you?'

After checking that all was well in the kitchen Tamily went into the drawing-room, where Dick was arranging drinks. She walked over to him and put her arms round his waist and hugged him.

'Lovely to see you, darling!' she whispered.

Dick put down the bottle-opener and gave her a quick return hug. He knew that she wanted to be kissed, but somehow he could not bring himself to do so—not after last night with Carol's kisses still burning his lips.

'How's things?' he asked quickly. 'It all looks very nice. Sorry to rush it on you, darling, but Harry Holmer's a pretty important client.'

Tamily smiled.

'I've got a nice lunch organized and, darling, we're having dinner here tonight and Sunday lunch at the Manor. You see, I'd already invited Adam Bond for tonight and...well, I couldn't very well put him off, could I?'

'That's okay!' Dick said, dropping his arms and turning away from Tamily's soft, loving gaze. He felt a nasty niggling guilt, knowing that *she* would never have behaved as he had done. Tamily was utterly loyal, completely his, body and soul. She wouldn't even *want* to be unfaithful...let alone give way to the urge.

'Well, it won't happen again!' he told himself sharply. But at the same moment he remembered the warm pressure of Carol's thigh pressed against his on the way down in the car from London; remembered that he had laughed and talked to her father and all the time he had wanted Carol desperately.

'You're very quiet, darling!' Tamily said behind him.

Dick's shoulders jerked. For a moment he had forgotten his wife's presence. He poured out a drink for her and turned to her, smiling;

'Tired, I expect. I worked pretty late last night.'

Tamily accepted his excuse without even the vaguest suspicion. Somehow it made him feel worse to realize how completely she trusted him.

Throughout the ensuing meal conversation was light-hearted and dominated by Carol's father. Although he was a little crude at times, Tamily liked him. He might be somewhat of a rough diamond—a self-made man—but he was honest and open and very kindly.

She was not quite so sure about his daughter Carol. Tamily did not like to be disparaging about anyone and yet Carol struck her as very opposite from her parent. She had a hard, brittle laugh and a polished sophistication which gave Tamily an acute feeling of inferiority. Although it was probably not intentional, there were several occasions when something Carol said could be taken two ways and the second way inferred that Tamily was a simpleton or a fool.

Then there was her proprietary way with Dick—almost as if he were there solely to dance attendance upon her. Tamily knew that, as host, Dick must look after her, but Carol was always needing something: a cigarette lit; a handbag left on a chair; a door shut or window opened.

'It's probably just the American way women have of bossing men around,' she told herself. But she did not like it; moreover, she was surprised that Dick showed no signs of objecting. As a rule, he was the one to do the asking. *'Oh, Tam, chuck that book over here! Tam, what about a drink? There's a couple of bottles of beer in the dining-room cupboard. Be a sport and fetch one.'*

After coffee they settled down in deckchairs in the garden and Tamily went upstairs to fetch Mercia. She put the little girl into a tiny primrose-yellow sundress in which she looked quite adorable. Fortunately Mercia had woken in a good mood and was eager to get downstairs to Daddy.

Dick, as always, made a great fuss of his little niece, hugging and kissing and teasing her until she was shouting with laughter. He introduced her to Carol, who surprised Tamily by allowing the child to play with her gold bracelet and fob chain and engaged her in conversation. Somehow Tamily had felt certain that the cool, stately American girl would not be interested in children.

Dick said proudly:

'She's a little minx. But we all adore her. She's a bit spoiled, of course, but not as badly as Tammy makes out!' He smiled at Tamily to take the sting from his words, but she was hurt none the less. The only arguments they'd ever had had been about Mercia's up-bringing and they'd become more heated as well as more frequent of late.

'I heard English women were strict disciplinarians!' Carol remarked in her drawl. 'In America we like our children to grow up natural.'

Dick eagerly agreed that this was the ideal. The complexes and inhibitions of civilization would come quickly enough —no need to hurry them on, he said.

Bored listening to their discussion on physiological development, Mercia moved on to Harry Holmer, who made almost as much fuss of her as Dick had done. He grinned across at Tamily and said:

'Reminds me of when Carol was knee-high to a grasshopper. Cute little monkey.

73

Reckon we spoiled her, too. Always had every little thing she wanted—still does, don't you, honey?'

Despite the intense warmth of the sunshine, Tamily felt a shiver of apprehension. Suppose Carol should want Dick?...but the idea was absurd. Dick was married now—no longer the eligible young man he had been in the days of Sylvia.... Tamily caught her breath sharply. *That's who Carol reminded her of!* Dick's old girl friend. She almost breathed a sigh of relief, realizing that Carol's likeness to Sylvia probably prompted her own unexplained antagonism to the American woman.

Sylvia—the half-Russian, half-French girl —had been Dick's first love. Although she was dark and Carol fair, they were much the same type—travelled, sophisticated, very much in charge of the situation and completely sure of themselves. Sylvia had been completely sure of Dick, too. But in the end she had chosen her wealthy French lover Pierre, and it hadn't taken Dick so very long to forget all about her. But Tamily had not forgotten. She had suffered so deeply at the time, loving Dick desperately and having to watch him in love with another girl.

She looked across at Dick with a great rush of gratitude and love. After three years of marriage she could still feel this wonder that he had married *her!* That he could love her. If no one else had been there she would have gone to him and touched his hand; told him how full of love she felt just at this very instant in time. But there was no opportunity until they were changing for dinner. Then, at last, they were alone in their bedroom.

Dick had removed his shirt and lay stretched out on the bed, his hands behind his head. He watched Tamily pull the cotton frock over her head and said:

'Gosh, I feel lazy. Too much sun! I could drop off for two pins.'

'You've got half an hour, darling,' Tamily told him. 'Why not have a quick sleep?'

She took off her underclothes and slipped into a thin cotton housecoat. Then she went over and sat down on the bed beside him.

Dick said:

'You look about fourteen in that thing. Funny little Tam!'

He reached up an arm and touched her tousled hair affectionately.

Tamily caught his hand and held it against her cheek.

'I love you so much!' she almost whispered. 'All afternoon I've been loving you so much.'

Dick swallowed. On any other occasion this would have been his cue to take her in his arms. As a rule they made love as soon as they were alone together at weekends; neither really able to relax and feel at ease until afterwards. But now—after last night with Carol...

Yet as he pulled Tamily down to him to kiss her he began to want her. Sensitive as she always was to every nuance of his feelings, she at once kissed him back passionately and he knew that he would make love to her after all. Even after three years of marriage her slim, boyish figure and soft sweetness excited and satisfied him. He knew her so well; their love-making was good and simple and honest. Maybe there was not the same intense excitement that Carol had evoked. Maybe the thrill of someone new was not there. But this need he had of Tammy was right; good; not just giving him an animal satisfaction of the body, but coloured and made beautiful because of the love he had for her and because she needed and loved him equally.

When it was over Dick lay silent, no longer sure of himself; once again hating himself. What kind of a man was he, wanting two women in as many days! What kind of a love was it that could be unfaithful so easily and meaninglessly?

'I'm sorry, Tam!' he thought, but he could not tell her. At least not now. Maybe one day he would. When it was all a long time in the past.

To his consternation Tamily said suddenly:

'Dick, do you find her attractive? Carol, I mean?'

He was glad that her head lay on his chest, her face turned away from him. He pushed a damp curl off her forehead and said as casually as possible:

'I suppose she is quite attractive!'

'She has a magnificent figure!' Tamily went on. 'Any man would notice that, surely?'

'She's a typical American girl—long and leggy!'

'But does she attract *you?*' Tamily persisted.

'What a ridiculous question—at a time

like this!' Dick prevaricated. 'Go and have your bath, Tam—or shall I go first?'

Reluctantly she left the safe haven of his arms. A few minutes ago she had been perfectly happy; perfectly at ease in mind and body. Now the same strange restlessness she had felt earlier was back.

Lying in the lukewarm water in the bath she tried to fathom the reason for her unease. Was she jealous of Carol? But that was silly. If there had been anything between the American girl and Dick he would never have made love just now. Just supposing he had been wanting the other girl, might he not have taken her, Tamily, as the next best thing? Even the thought horrified her. It was a beastly thing to think. The fact was, Tamily had nothing but instinct to guide her. There had never been another man in her life so she had no experience to help her think this out and discover the reasons for these strange thoughts. She felt that her fear was quite groundless—yet it existed, without a name.

She wondered suddenly whether this little fear was not, after all, just a by-product of a bigger one. For some time she had been faintly disturbed about her marriage. She had hated the weekly separation from Dick and been hurt because it did not seem to bother him at all. Was Dick falling out of love? Were three years of marriage sufficient to dull the novelty so that now he needed something more than just the farm and his young wife to enthrall him?

Tamily couldn't be sure of the answers to such questions. She had always known that Dick's love for her was of a different kind from her love for him. They were lovers as well as man and wife and yet except in the act of making love Dick was never totally hers—not as she, in her heart, belonged throughout each day and night to him. Her world and her happiness depended upon him. He had other interests; his love was more casual, taking everything for granted. He had never had for her that blind boyish adoration he'd once felt for Sylvia; nor even the intellectual understanding he had once shared with the girl from Oxford, Anthea, to whom he'd been engaged.

In the days of her own engagement to Dick and in the first year of marriage she had asked Dick again and again, 'But why do you love me?' And his answer had never varied: 'I don't know, Tam; you're you—a good friend, a good companion; you understand me. I just know I'm happy with you. It was the same when we were kids, wasn't it?'

It was enough—or had been. Why should she suddenly want something more now? Why should she suddenly feel that something was missing or lost?

She knew Dick would laugh at her fears if she were to tell him about them. He would accuse her of giving way to her old inferiority complex; of letting her imagination get the better of her common sense. And he was right. Dick hadn't changed in any way. She had nothing at all to fear.

'Buck up, Tam! You've been in there for hours. We'll be late at this rate!'

The familiar tone of his voice brought a swift smile to her eyes. No, Dick had not changed. There was nothing and no one to fear.

4

There was only an acre of garden surrounding Lower Beeches, but in the last three years Dick and Tamily worked like blacks to make it a little showpiece. Twice a week one of the manor house gardeners came down to do some of the rough work, but mostly the garden had been created by their own labours.

Proudly, Dick showed it to Carol as he walked her round before dinner. Immediately outside the house was an old flagstone terrace approached from the garden by a little brick path; either side of the path were standard rose trees, now in full bloom. To the left and right of these narrow beds were two emerald-green lawns flanked by beds of lavender which was sending out its pungent scent into the summer evening air.

For the most part the garden was made up of lawn with occasional unexpected beds of delphiniums and sweet-smelling pinks; with dwarf shrubs such as magnolia and azalea and some extra special scarlet and white camelia bushes. The whole garden was enclosed in a lovely old red brick wall on which grew peach and apple espaliers.

Carol bent and picked a camelia to fasten on her blue silk dress. With a provocative glance at Dick, she placed the scarlet flower in the low cleavage between her breasts. To the unsophisticated inhabitants of Allenton the dress would be shocking. Even Dick had been a little surprised at the lowness of the neck and the unembarrassed way in which Carol was exposing the top half of her body.

Seeing Dick's eyes on her, Carol smiled and said:

'I've not had a chance yet to say how much I enjoyed last night. May I come along to your flat and distract you again from your work?'

Dick flushed.

'I'm grateful for the suggestion, Carol, but I honestly don't think it's a good idea. I am a married man, you know, and now that you've met Tammy I'm sure you'll understand why I can't have an affair. She loves me very much and...well, I love her, too. I don't want to hurt her.'

It was Carol's turn to flush. She said shortly:

'Who's talking of love? You sound very old-fashioned, Dick. Are all Englishmen as strait-laced? Back home, even the happily marrieds have extra-marital relationships, as the books call it. I prefer to call it sex.'

They walked on slowly down to the end of the garden where the herbaccous border was a riot of colour. Dick said:

'Surely you want more than that, Carol? I mean, that kind of relationship doesn't offer you very much, does it? Don't you want to fall in love—get married?'

'When I meet the right man. Meanwhile, I see no reason why I shouldn't enjoy myself. It so happens I find you very exciting. Does my frankness shock you?'

It did, but Dick felt it would seem childish to admit it, he reminded himself that Carol was an American and that this was the possible explanation of her out-spokenness. All the same, he couldn't repeat last night's episode. However much he had enjoyed it at the time, it wasn't worth the horrible feeling of guilt he'd endured just now with Tamily. She would be so desperately hurt if she found out.

Not that she was likely to do so, tucked away down here while he and Carol...

'I'm sorry, Carol!' he said firmly because what half an hour ago seemed impossible now seemed all too probable. 'It isn't because I—I don't feel the same way about you. But there's Tam and—'

'Forget it, then, shall we?' Carol broke in sharply. 'My mistake. Somehow you don't look such a good boy, Dick. Your appearance is misleading.'

Dick's eyebrows went up.

'What does that mean, I wonder?'

Carol's lips twisted into a half-smile.

'You look as if you aren't afraid of anything or anyone; as if you aren't the kind to take orders from any woman—even your wife; as if you mean to get the best out of life by hook or by crook.'

They turned back towards the house. Dick was silent. The suggestion that he was being dull, ordinary, even cowardly, did not escape him. He wanted to argue the point. It had nothing to do with fear or being found out; or of taking orders from Tam or anyone else. It was just the way he felt...he didn't want to let Tam down. He loved her and he'd never do anything deliberately to hurt her....

Carol, too, was silent. She must not make the mistake of rushing Dick. Her instinct had been right so far; Dick had been married just long enough for the novelty to wear off. He was ripe for an affair, but she hadn't allowed for the fact that he didn't yet know that. Proximity and time would play the game her way. She could wait.

She rested a long, slim white hand on Dick's arm and said softly:

'That's okay by me, Dick. We'll stay friends—no sex, no complications.'

Relieved, Dick grinned down at her. He could afford now to pay her a compliment. He said:

'I should think being "just friends" with you, Carol, is a pretty unusual thing. Frankly, since we're being frank, you're the first woman I've met since I got married who made me even *want* to be unfaithful to my wife.'

'She's very sweet,' Carol remarked.

'Yes,' Dick agreed, glancing towards the terrace where Tamily was sitting between Adam Bond and Carol's father. Somehow the description 'sweet' coming from Carol also inferred that Tamily was a little dull. One day, when he had a chance, he would make Carol see that this wasn't true of Tam. She was his best friend, his 'pal', and there wasn't another woman in the world to equal her. He was suddenly glad that Tamily's dress was ordinary and not cut so low as to expose her breasts to the eyes of the man sitting beside her. Tam's figure might look boyish and unexciting now, but undressed...she was little and rounded and as responsive as he could have wished.

As they approached she looked up and smiled at them. Adam rose at once and introductions were made. After a brief glance at the tall, broad-shouldered man, Carol seated herself beside him. Here was exactly what she needed—another man to rouse Dick's jealousy.

'I've just been round the garden,' she said, looking straight into Adam's eyes. 'It's very lovely, isn't it?'

Tamily breathed a sigh of relief. She'd been afraid, since meeting Carol, that this dinner party was going to be a flop. Adam hardly struck her as Carol's type and she had imagined that with such a sophisticated woman he would be even more shy than usual.

As it was, he was soon in easy conversation with Carol, explaining about his work on the estate and saying how pleased he would be to escort her round the place next morning.

Tamily was able to give her attention to Mr Holmer, which was easy enough since he was prepared to do all the talking. It was, therefore, Dick who was 'odd man out'; having dispensed the drinks, he stood looking down at the foursome with an enigmatic stare. He was wishing, suddenly, that Tamily hadn't invited Adam Bond to dinner. Five was a bad number—not that anyone else seemed to be noticing it but himself. He watched Tamily smiling at Harry Holmer and was grateful. The man obviously liked her and Tam was a good listener. Then his eyes wandered to Carol and her companion and he realized for the first time what a good-looking chap Adam was. Taller than himself, broader and more mature. Carol seemed to like him—she was bending towards him with a cigarette between her lips. As the older man lit the match and held it to her, Dick saw Adam's eyes on Carol's low dress and was irritated. His irritation covered both of them. Carol was deliberately showing off her assets; and Adam ought to have more manners than to ogle her so obviously.

In point of fact Adam was not the least bit interested in Carol as a person. As Tamily had guessed, she was not his type. She frightened him with her hard, brittle voice and obvious desire to attract. At the same time he appreciated that she was a very beautiful female animal and very soon now the sight of a woman's figure would be something he could see only in his mind's eye. His awareness of beauty had increased a hundred-fold since he'd known how soon he was to be denied his vision. Yesterday, for the first time, he had noticed how pretty Tamily was and envied Dick. How opposite the two girls were, he thought. But young Allenton had good taste—he'd picked the right kind of girl for his wife. Tamily was as beautiful inside as the American girl was outside.

'I may call you Adam? It's such a satisfying name, I always think! And you must call me Carol!'

'She's a little bitch!' Dick thought. 'Out to attract anything in trousers. The less I see of her in future, the better.'

All the same, he found himself continuing to watch her throughout the meal with growing jealousy. He wondered if Carol would ever go to bed with a man like

Adam. She might—just for the novelty. He remembered again the feel of her body twisting and turning and wild with passion. He knew that there was something utterly primitive and yet strangely fascinating about the girl. It wasn't going to be so easy to keep on platonic terms. Maybe she knew that very well. He'd have to watch himself.

He wasn't aware that Tamily was watching him. Again and again as his eyes turned to Carol, Tamily saw and began to be afraid. She would have been blind not to realize how attractive the American looked in that low-cut dress. Even Adam stared at her from time to time. But Dick seemed unable to keep his eyes off her.

Tamily felt like crying. In a way she couldn't blame Dick for noticing the girl...but not long ago he had been making love to her. It was almost as if she were being forced to watch him being unfaithful.

Abruptly she asked Mr Holmer how long they were staying in London.

'A few weeks, I guess. Depends when the deal goes through. And, of course, on how soon my little girl gets bored. Carol never stays any place for long. Restless—that's what I tell her. When she gets to my age she won't feel so goddam' anxious to chase around the globe—pardon my language, honey!'

A few weeks! Tamily thought. Would they stay in London? Would she be seeing Dick? Silently she prayed that Carol would soon get bored and decide to move on.

After dinner Dick suggested he should take the Holmers up to the manor house for coffee with his parents. Tamily, knowing that this might be slightly embarrassing for Adam, excused herself from going on the grounds that Mercia might wake and call for her.

'Adam will stay and keep me company,' she said as Dick started to argue.

Dick looked at his wife with slight annoyance. The fact was, he felt Carol might be bored just sitting around talking after dinner. Allenton Manor would interest her and he was longing to show off his childhood home. But Tamily refusing to come split up the party. Having to 'baby-mind' Mercia was clearly only an excuse not to go with them, and he jumped to the wrong conclusion that she had taken a dislike to Carol and was openly showing it. It never occurred to him that she had refused on Adam's behalf.

But he could not argue the point in front of his guests, and after phoning through to his mother to say he was on his way, he left with the Holmers, leaving Tamily and Adam alone.

'Are you sure you didn't want to go?' Adam asked quietly.

'Yes, of course!' Tamily said, sitting down opposite him in the drawing-room, now strangely quiet and peaceful after the departure of the others. She drew a big sigh and stretched herself out more comfortably. 'It's nice to relax for a bit!' She was suddenly very tired and unaccountably depressed.

Adam watched her speculatively.

'Do you find entertaining a strain?'

She smiled up at him.

'Not really—or, at least, not when it's my own friends. But...'

'I know. Miss Holmer is a bit nerve-racking!'

The remark was so unlike Adam that Tamily stared at him and then grinned.

'That's just about it. She's very attractive to look at.'

'And dangerous.'

Again Tamily was surprised.

'In what way?'

'Rich, bored and beautiful. Surely the ingredients that make for danger. I wouldn't trust her further than I could see her.'

Suddenly conscious that he had been rude about one of Tamily's guests, he flushed and started to apologize. But Tamily interrupted.

'You don't have to be sorry. I feel the same way about her. But I thought I might be being catty—you know, feminine jealousy because she's so beautiful and because my husband obviously thinks so too.'

'I don't think you need worry about Dick. He is not likely to stray very far with a wife as pretty as yourself around the home.'

It was Tamily's turn to flush. Compliments from Adam! He was acting quite out of character. As a rule he was very formal and never intimate. At the same time his remark was consoling. He was a man and if he didn't like Carol as a person, maybe Dick...?

'May I smoke my pipe?' Adam asked. 'I know you said you didn't mind last time I was here.'

'No, of course not. I like the smell of a pipe.'

She watched him fill and light it and thought:

'How relaxed and at ease he is. Funny that I never noticed before what a restful, easy person he is to be with.' Her own nervous system seemed to have been strung tight ever since she had heard Dick was bringing home weekend guests. Now, she too, was relaxing and the tiredness was going.

'Are you really going to take Miss Holmer round the estate tomorrow?' she asked into the silence.

Adam smiled.

'Why not? It'll get her out of your way in the morning and I have to go round, anyway. Don't you think I should?'

Tamily laughed—a gay, carefree laugh.

'She won't be able to go far in those shoes. I'll have to lend her some low-heeled ones. Will you walk—or drive?'

'Walk!' Adam said, smiling back at her. 'I'll tire her out.'

They laughed together, like conspirators.

It was only then that Tamily suddenly remembered the terrible threat that hung over this man's head. Yet he appeared quite normal and could even laugh.

'I think you are very brave!' she said impulsively. 'Anyone else in your position would be filled with self-pity and depression.'

It was a moment or two before he realized she was referring to his threatened blindness. The smile left his face as he said:

'I'm learning to live with the knowledge. In a strange way it has made life more enjoyable. I am beginning to see everything around me as if I had completely new eyes...the way an artist would, I suppose. I notice tiny details and imprint all that is beautiful on my mind's eye to remember later. Your dress, for instance—the blue flowers on it like cornflowers; the way the twilight is falling in this room, softening everything and blurring outlines. On the way here I noticed dandelions growing in the ditch and spiders crawling in the dust of the lane. It's almost as if I've just been given my sight. Strange!'

'And aren't you frightened—of the future?'

'Yes! I try not to think about anything but "now". That way I can enjoy each day I have left. I'm not nearly as brave as you might suppose, though. I have moments of great depression.'

'You ought not to be alone!' Tamily cried. 'If you feel wretched will you promise to come and see me? You don't have to ring or wait for an invitation—just drop in. I'm nearly always here, as you know. Maybe just having someone to talk to would help.'

'That's extremely kind of you. I hope you'll drop in on me, too, more often than you have done in the past. And bring little Mercia. Once I used to think I'd love a little daughter just like her.'

The moment was so full of nostalgia that Tamily said quickly:

'Not just like Mercia. She's a spoilt little imp. I'm sorry you never knew her mother, Adam. You'd have loved her—everyone did. She was really an angel. Do you know, she was a semi-invalid nearly all her childhood and yet one never heard her complain. She was the most unselfish person I ever knew!'

'You loved her very much?'

'Yes, I did. And Dick adored her. That's why he spoils little Mercia—he just can't refuse the child anything. But she hasn't her mother's nature. I don't think you *could* have spoiled Dick's sister; whereas this little bundle of mischief takes advantage whenever you give her the barest chance.'

'Bring her to tea next week. I'll keep her in order.'

Tamily laughed.

'I expect you would, too. Children aren't so different from little animals and they sense who is boss. I think Mercia might have a healthy respect for you.'

They finished coffee and at Adam's request Tamily put on some records. She and Dick had a wide range of 'pops', but Tamily also had some opera which she loved and it was these arias she played now.

She was not to know the effect this was to have on Adam. The combination of romantic songs, perfectly sung in the twilight of a summer evening—a young, pretty woman moving quietly and gracefully to and from the radiogram—all conspired to produce in him a sudden painful realization of what he had missed in life. This could be *his* home—*his* wife; this evening could be one of many they shared, their charming, mischievous little daughter asleep upstairs. With so much, the loss of his sight would not have been so terrible a blow.

'Tamily!' he thought, as the strains of the love song from *La Bohème* struck an answering chord deep in his heart. 'If you were not Allenton's wife I could have loved you. If I let myself...'

But he clamped quickly on the thought. Love was not for him—nor ever would be now. And Tamily was already married to a boy her own age and to one who had far, far more to offer her. Dick was a nice enough boy, too. Just so long as he made Tamily happy—

The sound of a car in the drive broke in on his thoughts.

Tamily stood up quickly, saying: 'Blast! Now we'll have to give up.' She switched on two table-lamps and went across the room. Surprise in her voice, she said: 'Why, we were sitting in the dark! I never noticed. It's been a lovely evening, Adam. We must do it again. I didn't know you were as fond as I am of opera.'

The front door opened, and Carol's voice, gay and strident, broke in upon them. Tamily and Adam exchanged glances, indicating how sorry they were that their peaceful enjoyment had come to an end.

Dick stood in the doorway, looking at each of them in turn.

'We thought you must have gone to bed, Tam. There were no lights on as we came towards the house.'

Tamily blushed. She was embarrassed as well as angry. Dick made it sound as if she and Adam...

'We were listening to some of my records,' she said. 'We didn't notice how dark it was until we heard the car.'

Adam was on his feet, holding out his hand to Dick.

'Time I was off,' he said. 'Thank you both very much for a pleasant evening. What time shall I see you tomorrow, Miss Holmer?'

Carol's amused eyes glanced across at him.

'Whenever you say.'

The appointment was made for 10.30 and then Adam was gone. After a quick nightcap Tamily followed Dick upstairs to bed.

Alone in the bedroom, Dick said sullenly:

'What's got into you, Tam? Are you sulking or something? First you refuse to come up to the manor with us; then you create a highly embarrassing moment by mooching in the dark with Bond.'

Tamily pulled her dress over her head and said angrily:

'I don't know what you mean by "mooching". We were listening to records —and as to it being embarrassing, you were the one to make it so by inferring that we'd been up to something!'

Dick's face relaxed.

'Keep your hair on! I know you weren't up to anything. But the others might have thought—'

'What might they have thought?' Tamily burst out, suddenly quite furious. 'And who cares, anyway? It's not my fault if Carol Holmer has a dirty mind.'

Dick went on smiling. He was enjoying the sight of Tamily's angry face and flashing eyes. It amused him to see her in a temper.

'Well, you must admit it did look odd, suddenly switching on the lights when you heard the car.'

'Shut up!' Tamily said. 'It's horrid even to talk like that. It just shows how little you know about Adam. Why, he—'

'Pack it up, Tam. I was only teasing!' Dick broke in, going across the room to put his arms round her.

She twisted out of his embrace, her voice still angry. 'No, I won't. Maybe you are just teasing or maybe you want to make me angry to cover up for your own misdeeds. Don't think I didn't notice the way you were looking at Carol all through dinner. Maybe people living in glass houses shouldn't throw stones.'

The smile fell away from Dick's face and he glanced at Tamily's white face speculatively. Was this just a shot in the dark or did she know something? Had he or Carol betrayed themselves? He felt guilty and angry with Tamily for making him so.

'You're obviously in a stinking mood!' he said, turning away. 'Under the circumstances we'll terminate the conversation.'

'So you don't deny it?' Tamily asked quietly. She was suddenly very much afraid. Her taunt at Dick had been no more than a method of getting back at him for spoiling what had been such a lovely evening with Adam; but the expression on his face when she had suggested that he, in turn, had been misbehaving had given her own thoughtless jibe far greater significance. Now she really was jealous—though of what she had yet to find out.

'I don't know what you are talking about!' Dick replied. 'For heaven's sake let's drop this ridiculous quarrel and get to bed.'

'Then you do find her attractive?'

'So what? Is that a crime?'

'Not if that's all there is to it.'

'Well, what more could there be?' Dick lied swiftly. 'After all, I am a married man.'

He marched off into the bathroom, leaving Tamily alone and even more frightened than before. It wasn't that she suspected him of having been unfaithful to her; it was the frustrated tone of voice in which he had just declared his married status. He had sounded so resentful—so *un*pleased. It was like a slap in the face.

She sat down at the dressing-table and began to brush her hair. She wanted to climb into bed, pull the bedclothes over head and shut out the world—the way she had used to do as a child when she had been afraid of unknown terrors of the dark. But she hadn't yet washed or done her teeth and Dick was in the bathroom. Tonight she couldn't share it with him.

He came out presently, his hair curling from the steam of his bath water, his face young and showing no sign of fatigue. He glanced across at her, noticing how she averted her eyes, and said:

'Come on, Tam. It's nearly midnight!'

His voice sounded ordinary, unstrained. Tamily clung to the thought that everything that had been said was only in her imagination. It had been a stupid quarrel about nothing—Dick had got over his bad mood and she had only to climb out of hers and all would be well between them. When she got into bed beside him he would put his arms round her and he would prove with his love how much he enjoyed being a married man.

But it wasn't like that. As she slipped in between the sheets Dick made no move to put his arms round her. His breathing came deep and regularly, as if he were asleep, but somehow she knew that he was feigning. Pride forbade that she should speak to him or make the first move towards a reconciliation. It wasn't up to her to prove her love for him—he was, as he had always been, quite sure of her.

The minutes ticked by and the silence was broken only by the striking of midnight from the church clock.

His eyes shut, but very wide awake, Dick was thinking:

'I dare not touch her. Somehow she has guessed. Tam's far more sensitive than I thought. I shall have to be more careful—damned careful! I don't want her to be hurt.'

Only then did he realize that deep down inside he had admitted to himself that there was a chance of his hurting her a second time.

5

Sunday was a day of complete frustration
and irritation for Tamily. She woke tired,
her nerves still on edge. The reconciliation
with Dick seemed even further away. Both
talked in short, stilted sentences, as if they
were strangers. It was so unlike their usual
Sunday mornings. As a rule they woke in
each other's arms to enjoy a long, lazy
lie-in while Sandra dressed Mercia and
breakfasted the child in the kitchen before
bringing up their breakfast on a tray.

Because of the Holmers this morning's
breakfast would be in the dining-room and
Dick gave instructions to Sandra, when
she brought their early-morning tea, that
Mercia should have hers with them.

'Do you think that's a good idea?'
Tamily asked when Sandra departed.

Dick frowned. 'Why ever not? I'll see
she behaves!'

But when breakfast-time came it was
Tamily who had to try to keep an
effervescent child quiet and prevent her

104

from tipping soft-boiled egg-yolk over her lap and the tablecloth.

'Don't keep on at her!' Dick said once angrily. 'If she doesn't want to eat it let her go without!'

'We never force kids to eat in the States,' Carol said smoothly.

Tamily bit down her angry reply. She knew very well that Mercia would have eaten her egg and enjoyed it in other circumstances. This was the child showing off, trying to attract attention to herself and succeeding admirably.

Meaning well, Mr Holmer took Mercia on his lap and fed her snippets of buttered toast. Mercia shot Tamily a triumphant look—one of purely feminine triumph.

For the remainder of the morning she ran riot, shouting, laughing, getting in everybody's way. When Carol and Dick left to meet Adam the laughter turned to howls as she realized she could not go, too.

'It's too far for you to walk, Poppet,' Dick tried to explain, but Mercia wasn't interested in reasons. She had had her own way so far and she wasn't going to give up lightly now.

Tamily tried to cope while she helped

Sandra make beds and wash up after breakfast. Mercia whined continually until Tamily slapped her. At once the child's angelic little face creased into a furious frown.

'You naughty!' she said. 'Mercia tell Daddy. Daddy be cross with you!'

Tamily felt like crying.

'Don't you worry, M'm,' Sandra said consolingly. 'She'll quieten down when you're at the Manor.'

But, as Mercia had foretold, Dick was angry with Tamily for slapping her. As they tidied up before going to lunch he said:

'She's only a tot, Tamily. You've no right to take your own temper out on her. It shows a complete lack of self-control!'

Tamily's face was fiery red with indignation.

'Then why didn't you stay home and "manage" her, if you're so good at it? It was all your fault, anyway—getting her over-excited. You spoil her.'

'The trouble with you is you are jealous!'

Tamily gasped. Dick's voice had been cold, emotionless. In fact, he had not really meant what he had said. He knew deep down that he was partly to blame for the child's bad behaviour. But he was beginning to resent the way Tamily was always managing to make him feel guilty. It was getting tiresome, to say the least of it.

'You'd better apologize, Dick. That was a beastly thing to say—and quite untrue!'

'For heaven's sake!' Dick broke in. 'It's nearly one o'clock. We'll be late!'

Because of his annoyance with Tamily, Dick went out of his way to be attentive and charming to Carol at lunchtime. Tamily tried to talk to her mother-in-law, but she was kept busy most of lunchtime listening to Mr Holmer. Lord Allenton, with Carol on his right, was too far from Tamily to converse with her. So she remained silent and, noticing it from time to time, Dick presumed she was sulking.

'Two can play at that game!' he told himself, and for the rest of the afternoon he behaved as if Tamily were not even there.

Soon after tea the Holmers were ready to drive back to Town. Mercia, laughing and happy again after her afternoon's sleep, clung to his legs and said:

'Daddy stay. Please, Daddy!'

'I can't, Precious!' Dick said, hugging her. He looked over the top of the child's head and met Tamily's eyes, large, unhappy and, he imagined, resentful.

'Daddy has to work very hard!' he said flatly. 'You be a good girl and stay here with Mummy.'

Tamily stood stiffly while he bent and kissed her cheek. She had hoped all afternoon that somehow Dick would manage a moment alone with her before he left. They couldn't part with this nameless stupid misunderstanding between them.

She deliberately lingered over his packing, hoping he would come up to their room, take her in his arms and tell her not to be such a silly chump. But he had not come and her hopes had given way to a mixture of pride and despair.

'I'll ring you!' were the only words he said, and then stooped to pick up his own and Carol's suitcases to take them out to the waiting car.

Carol's goodbye was cool and assured.

'So kind of you to entertain us. Perhaps you'll be up in London soon, so we can return your hospitality? I'll get Dick to fix a date, shall I?'

It was almost as if Dick were *her* husband, Tamily thought furiously.

But her anger departed soon after the car

had disappeared down the lane. With the returning quiet, depression took full hold of her. It was always like this on a Sunday when Dick left—but this time it was almost unbearable to be left alone—the new hateful barrier cutting Dick off even more effectively than the growing miles of distance.

She began to blame herself. Jealousy was an ugly emotion and she *had* been jealous of Carol Holmer. Even if she had not openly expressed her feelings Dick had noticed and been hurt by her lack of trust in him. The quarrel was all her fault!

With Dick's departure, Mercia had once again lost her good spirits and there was a scene when Tamily told her it was bedtime. Jess, arriving in the middle of it, noticed Tamily's white strained face and said:

'I'll put her to bed. Why don't you go and sit in the garden for a while? It's still warm and you look worn out.'

'I'm not in the least tired...' Tamily began, and then smiled. She was behaving just like Mercia! 'Thanks, Mother. I think I'll go for a walk. I might look on Adam Bond. I promised last night to lend him some of my good records, but I forgot to give them to him.'

'He'll be glad of some company, I expect,' Jess agreed. 'I don't altogether like the look of him since his operation. I reckon there's more wrong than he lets on.'

It was on the tip of Tamily's tongue to explain, but she remembered her promise to Adam and refrained.

'I won't be long,' she said.

She collected the records and, flinging a white cardigan round her shoulders, walked off down the lane towards the drive and Adam's cottage.

He was in the garden tying up ramblers and did not notice her at first. She stood watching him, heard him swear mildly as he pricked his finger, and laughed. He swung round, his face breaking into a smile of welcome.

'How very nice to see you. I've just about had this job. Come in and have a drink. Have the others gone back to Town?'

As the minutes ticked by, Tamily began to relax. She sat quietly, listening to him talking in his slow, deep voice and thought with surprise, 'Why, he's my friend!'

'I'll take great care of the records. Do you have to hurry back or could we play some of them now?'

Tamily explained that her mother had just dropped in for an hour and was putting Mercia to bed.

'It's Sandra's evening off, so I'll have to get back to Mercia,' she said regretfully. 'Perhaps I could come another time?'

Adam looked at her eagerly. It was wonderful for him to have company. Any human being would be welcome and Tamily...well, in some strange way she was someone very special.

'Tomorrow? I could return the dinner —not that I'm much of a cook, but I bagged a hare yesterday morning and it should be just right for jugging. That's one meal I can cook.'

Tamily nodded appreciatively.

'I'd love it. I'll have to go now. I'll see you about seven.'

She walked home, amazed that she should be feeling so much better. With all tension gone, her spirits had risen unpredictably.

'I'll ring Dick at the flat—tell him I'm sorry I was so moody!' she thought 'Then everything will be all right.'

Dick, apparently, had had the same idea. Jess told her daughter he had phoned while she was out. Tamily's face flushed with pleasure. So Dick wanted to 'make up', too.

'I'll ring him back!' she said joyfully. But Jess shook her head.

'He's going out to dine with the Holmers and probably won't be back very early. He said just to give you his love.'

Jess eyed her daughter shrewdly. Obviously something was wrong between her and Dick.

'Want to tell me what's up?' she asked gently.

Tears of disappointment filled Tamily's eyes. She brushed them away and attempted a smile.

'I expect I'm being very silly. It's that horrible American girl, Mother. I'm sure she had her hooks into Dick and he...well, I just don't know for *sure* if I can trust him.'

Jess was silent. She'd known Dick since he was a small boy; known just what a madcap he had been; a lover of fun and danger and variety. There'd been the usual childish escapades and, later, love affairs which had come to nothing.

It had seemed when he married Tamily as if he were willing to settle down, his wild oats sown, to domestic happiness and responsibility. But now she wondered if a man of Dick's type ever did settle down completely. Three years of marriage was long enough for the first happy shine of novelty to wear thin; long enough for Dick to become restless, a little bored perhaps.

'You've no reason not to trust him?' she asked thoughtfully.

'No facts—just instinct. I don't even know if I *do* suspect him. But suddenly everything has gone wrong, and it's because of Carol Holmer. I know she's trying to attract him and...Mother, she's a very attractive girl. She makes me feel country-cousin and about as unsophisticated as a field mouse!'

Jess smiled.

'Dick married you because you were the type he wanted for his wife. If he had preferred sophistication he'd never have picked on you, would he? At the same time, darling, there's no reason why you shouldn't put on a new face—you know, buy a few smart clothes and get your hair re-styled—just for a change.'

Tamily's face brightened.

'That might be fun. I could go up to London—do one of those quick-change tricks you see in magazines—Before and After. Perhaps I will—I'll go this week and then next weekend I'll surprise Dick.'

After her mother had said good night and promised to take over Mercia the following Friday, Tamily went to bed in a happier frame of mind. She was even a little excited as she elaborated on the idea of changing her appearance and saw in her imagination Dick's expression when he discovered his 'new' wife.

She would not have been so happy if she could have seen Dick at that moment, quietly letting Carol into his flat.

He switched on the standard lamp and flung his jacket over the back of a chair, then helped Carol out of her pale blue coat. As her arms came free she turned and twisted them round his neck, bringing her mouth hard against his. When he released her she was breathing deeply and smiling at him.

'I've been aching to do that all weekend. It was quite a strain keeping my distance.'

He kissed her again, roughly, hurting her, and said:

'You shouldn't be here. It's dangerous—unfair...if Tam—'

'Forget her!' Carol whispered, her fingers warm against the back of his neck. 'She won't know. Besides, danger is exciting. You know you love it.'

'Yes!' he thought. 'I love it and I want her and she knows it.' Aloud he said:

'I'm not in the least in love with you, Carol. I'm not even sure that I like you very much.'

She threw back her head and laughed delightedly.

'Good! That means you're afraid of me.'

The taunt struck home.

'The hell I am!' he said hoarsely, and took her back into his arms.

It was all over very soon, Carol, as before, fiercely demanding and quickly satisfied. For Dick it was exciting, but when his passion was spent there came once more the haunting memory of Tamily's hurt little face and large unhappy eyes. Carol's voice, lazy and contented, dispelled thought.

'Honey, I've been thinking about your farm—the money you need to get started. I suppose it would be useless to offer you what you want—as a gift, I mean?'

115

Dick sat up, his face shocked and angry.

'Good God, yes! As if I'd take money from *you!*'

Carol smiled.

'Okay—don't hit the roof. It wasn't meant as an insult. It's just that I have plenty and—'

'No, Carol. Forget it!'

'I could buy shares in the property, couldn't I? Be a sleeping partner?' She gave him a wicked, provocative smile.

Dick relaxed and touched her bare shoulders gently. 'Thanks, Carol, but anything like that is out. Right out.'

Carol sat up, throwing her head back to get the blonde hair away from her face. She lit a cigarette and blew the smoke out of her mouth thoughtfully.

'Remember I told you I'd find out about this big deal? It's a merger, Dick; American-British firms. You can safely put in all the capital you have, and on Dad's reckoning the shares will be double before the autumn when news of the merger breaks.'

Dick looked down at her eagerly.

'That I do go for. Not, damn it, that I've much capital to put in. Fifteen hundred is probably the most I could raise. Still,

116

double that and I'm not so far off my five-thousand-pound target.'

Carol watched Dick's face thoughtfully. He was waiting for her to tell him the names of the firms—but he wasn't having the information for free. She wanted something in exchange and wasn't too sure how to put it. She said softly:

'Dick, I want very much to have a long weekend in Cannes. I'm an inveterate gambler, you know, and I'm dying to get to the casino. I don't want to go alone and Daddy says he can't leave London yet awhile. Do you think you could escort me? I'd pay all expenses, of course.'

Dick drew in his breath. He told himself Carol's last remark had nothing to do with her earlier one about the merger. It was just that her mind had swung from one thing to another. It wasn't meant to be a pay-off. All the same, how could he go? What sensible reason could he give Tam for shooting off to the South of France with another woman—one she didn't like, at that!

As if guessing the reason for his hesitation, Carol said quickly:

'It might be wiser to let your wife

think Pop was coming; say a bit about the possible merger and what it might mean to you financially to keep Dad happy.'

Dick relaxed. Carol wasn't 'buying' him—the merger was just to provide the excuse for him to go. In a way he'd love it. He hadn't been abroad for years, and Cannes—the casino—with a woman like Carol...

'I'd like it, you know that. It's just —damn it, Carol, I have to remember I'm married. It's all very well for you—you aren't answerable to anyone else. Besides, what would your father say if he found out?'

'Don't worry about Dad. All he wants is for me to be happy. He'll turn a blind eye if I tell him not to ask any questions. No need to commit yourself at this stage if you don't want to, honey. Think about it and let me know.'

It was only after she had left his flat that Dick remembered she hadn't yet given him the names of the shares he should buy. She must have forgotten, he told himself. He'd ask her tomorrow when he took her out to lunch.

He took a quick bath and fell into bed.

Within minutes he was sound asleep—a long refreshing sleep unhaunted by memories of Carol or his wife's questioning, unhappy face.

6

'You look lovely—*lovely!*' Adam Bond repeated as Tamily stood shyly in front of him. She had that afternoon returned from London with new hair-style, new clothes and, for the first time in her life, a professional make-up. This last item had been an afterthought. She had made up her mind on the spur of the moment to agree with her hairdresser's suggestion that she have a facial to complete the transformation.

Fortunately for Tamily, the woman who had given her the facial had recognized Tamily's beauty as being of the open-air, natural kind. She had given her the lightest of foundations, a pale lipstick and not too much eye make-up. The big difference had been made when she had plucked Tamily's rather thick, dark eyebrows. Somehow, by doing so, it made her face look more delicate and accentuated the oval shape and large eyes.

Tamily had nearly lost her nerve on the

train to London that morning. Only her mother's encouragement had made her keep to her plan. But with the new rather Eastern-looking silk dress and matching coat, the new forward curling fringe of hair across her forehead, the new face, she was suddenly thrilled and excited. Now she knew that she could stand up beside Carol Holmer without feeling inferior.

A little of her belief in her new self ebbed on the train home. On a sudden impulse she stopped at the Lodge on the way home to see what Adam's reactions were. The new-found friendship with Adam Bond had come about so spontaneously and naturally that Tamily had not been conscious of its sudden blossoming. Since the weekend she had spent two evenings with him playing records and he had been up to the house for tea with her and Mercia. With Adam she had no feeling of shyness, of self-consciousness, and he never gave her the slightest feeling of inferiority. Adam was quiet, gentle, kind and there was no conscious effort to entertain him; he seemed happy enough just to enjoy her company and little Mercia's.

She looked at him now with a pleased smile.

'I'm so glad you approve!' she said eagerly. 'I was afraid you might think it ghastly—or not "me", or something. I can't wait for Dick to come tomorrow and to see if he likes me like this!'

She twisted on one foot like a small girl, becoming at once the 'old' Tamily, natural, unspoilt. Adam Bond drew in his breath sharply.

One week had been enough for him to fall hopelessly and painfully in love with her. He knew that she did not even notice him as a man and he was glad of it. Had his feelings been in the least obvious to her their new-found friendship would have been impossible. He was far too honest a man even to speak of love to another man's wife—and especially not Dick Allenton's, whom he looked on a part friend, part employer. His love and awareness of Tamily was a secret for ever buried in his heart.

But he could not hide it from himself, and the pain was in the knowledge that she had made herself beautiful, not for him, but for Dick. But his jealousy was passive and he was happy for Tamily because she was happy. The big difficulty was to hide from her just how beautiful he thought she was—not only now when she seemed so strangely grown-up all of a sudden, but when she was knocking round in her old cotton skirt or shorts, her slim brown legs in their sandals like a schoolgirl's, her hair tousled and untidy like a boy's.

'Time for a drink before you go home?' he asked lightly.

Tamily smiled.

'All right! I ought to get back, really, but I'd love a long, cool something. It was frantically hot in Town. I'd *hate* to live in London, wouldn't you, Adam? I don't know how Dick can stand the flat in summer.'

She followed him into the house and watched him pour out a lime-juice for her and a beer for himself. They took the drinks into the garden and sat in silence, sipping them. This was one of the pleasant things about their friendship—they could sit without feeling the need of talking.

Presently Tamily stood up and said with regret:

'I'd better go. Shall I see you tomorrow, Adam? Dick should be home for lunch. Perhaps you'd like to come up for tea?'

He shook his head. He wanted to go. All the time now he felt the need to be near her, within sound of her voice; most of all to have her in his vision to remember.... But she had once told him how she treasured her weekends alone with Dick and he had no intention of intruding.

'Got a lot of work to do!' he said vaguely. 'Perhaps Monday.'

He tried to get down to the farm accounts after she had left but he could not concentrate. Monday was two whole days away.

'This is madness,' he told himself sharply. At his age he should know the folly of crying for the moon. Even if Tamily had been unmarried he could not have dreamed of marrying her. A blind man was useless and no good to any woman. There could be no hope, and because of that he must make up his mind quite firmly to treasure what he did have and guard it carefully—her friendship.

He could not help wondering how Dick could bear to be parted from his young wife all week. In Dick's shoes Adam would have preferred to commute, however boring the journey. At least there would be the nights....

He closed his mind quickly against the sudden unbearable longing to feel Tamily's slim youthful body in his arms. It had been such a long time since he had wanted a woman, and now desire, the close companion to the newly discovered love, was an intense burning need which he found hard to suppress.

He was quite unprepared for the sudden reappearance of the girl who was so much in his thoughts. He heard her banging on the front door, then her voice called to him and a moment later she burst into the room. Her face was chalk-white, her eyes even more enormous.

He rose at once and put a steadying hand on her arm.

'What's wrong? Tell me, Tamily!'

His voice calmed her at once. She had come running down here near to hysteria—a state of emotion quite foreign to her.

Adam pushed her gently into a chair and said again:

'Tell me what has happened, Tamily.'

'Oh, Adam!' Her voice was full of her shocked unhappiness. 'It's Dick—he isn't coming down this weekend.'

He almost smiled in his relief. Then, seeing the expression in her eyes, he waited. Slowly the words came:

'He's going to the South of France—with *her,* Carol Holmer. They are having four days in Cannes, together—flying first thing tomorrow morning. Adam, how could he, how *could* he?'

Quite suddenly she was crying and his arms went round her as if it were the most natural thing in the world. She buried her face against his shoulder and sobbed out her disappointment.

'It's so unfair!' she said in a muffled, unhappy little voice. 'He ought to have let me know—I'd never have gone up to Town today if I'd known. And he hasn't even asked me if I'd like to go, too.'

Adam stroked her hair, his heart beating so loud he was afraid she would hear it. As soon as he could, he released himself from the dangerous proximity to her. She sat down again, sniffing into her handkerchief, reminding him again of a little girl.

'My dear, you mustn't get so upset. I'm sure Dick would not be going without you if it were possible to take you. It's probably all tied up with business, isn't it?'

Tamily grimaced. Already the first shock was wearing off. Now she was no longer angry—just miserable.

'Not really! He wrote last night to

126

explain, but I caught the early train this morning so I missed the early post. The letter was waiting when I got back just now. Oh, Adam, it's *so* disappointing. I wanted to surprise him—'

She broke off, staring down at the new outfit, touching her now-tousled hair with a rueful glance.

Adam said:

'Maybe he prefers you the way you usually look. There's nothing to get so upset about. You're over-tired, I think.'

'London *was* ghastly,' Tamily agreed. She tried to smile. 'I suppose I'm being rather childish. The fact is, Adam, I'm just plain jealous. Carol Holmer is very attractive and—'

'I refuse to believe Dick is in the least interested in her. And you're his *wife,* Tamily.'

She nodded.

'All the same, he noticed her. You did, too, didn't you, Adam?'

He shrugged.

'Oh, yes, I noticed her. But that most certainly isn't the type of woman I could want.'

But even as he spoke he was no longer believing the reassurance he gave her. Carol

Holmer was one hundred per cent the kind of woman a man would enjoy making love to—and Dick might be momentarily attracted. Four days alone with such a woman in Cannes....

'Mr Holmer is going, too, of course,' Tamily sighed. 'So I suppose I'm making a mountain out of a molehill. But it doesn't really make sense, Adam. Dick says he has to go because Mr Holmer is going to let him in on some share deal or something and he dare not offend him by refusing. It's a kind of blackmail, isn't it? But Dick says it may mean all the difference between starting the farm next year and not having to wait for four or five.'

'Well, there you are, then. He's only thinking of you—long term. I agree it has a nasty smell—but most big business has. That's the way of a lot of "deals" are pulled off—by keeping the right people happy.'

This time the smile really did reach Tamily.

'You are a great comfort, Adam!' she said. 'Already I feel much better about it. I also feel ashamed of myself for being such an embarrassment to you. After I'd

128

read the letter I didn't stop to think. I just ran back here.'

Adam's face was suddenly taut.

'I'm glad you came to me. That's what friends are for. And you and I are friends, aren't we?'

She nodded.

'Yes! It's strange, isn't it, Adam, how it has happened quite suddenly? We've been within a half-mile of each other for nearly three years and yet it's only this last two weeks that we've really got to know each other. I was rather shy of you before. Seems silly now.'

'That's the way love comes, suddenly and unexpectedly, with no warning or discrimination!' Adam told himself. Aloud he said:

'Maybe this is one of God's compensations for my approaching blindness—that I should suddenly find friends.'

'Oh, Adam, you make me feel ashamed. I've been carrying on like a spoilt child because I'm thwarted and disappointed, but you face up to something really frightening with quiet calm and courage.'

'I'm not in the least calm or courageous,' Adam replied. 'At times I'm scared stiff. I try *not* to remember and that shows a complete lack of courage. I ought to be able to face up to it—not try to hide it from everyone as well as myself.'

Tamily stood up. This time it was she who laid a hand on his arm. She said softly:

'You haven't hidden it from me. I'm glad. You'll let me help when you're feeling bad, won't you? After all, that's what friends are for.'

He nodded, knowing that he would fight hard against the desire for her sympathy, her pity, her understanding. He could not claim these in the name of friendship when he wanted them so badly in the name of love.

'Do you ever read poetry?' Tamily was asking him. 'If you don't know it you should read John Milton's poem *On His Blindness*. And the other one of his called *Light*. He learned to live with darkness. I'll lend you my book, if you like.'

'I'll come up to the house tomorrow and borrow it. Maybe I could come to tea after all? I don't see why I shouldn't indulge myself a little, do you?'

Tamily's face brightened, just as he had hoped it would.

'Oh, Adam, will you? The weekend is

going to seem so dull and I know I'll only get depressed on my own. Let's take a picnic tea to the bluebell wood. Mercia would love that and it'll be cooler there than in the garden. Would it bore you?'

'Of course not. I'll try and be there before four.'

But the temporary relief from disappointment did not last when Tamily was back in the empty house. Mercia was sleeping the night up at the Manor with Jess; Sandra had gone home. Lower Beeches seemed suddenly very large, very solitary.

Tamily had a quick supper off the tray Sandra had left in the kitchen and went up to bed. Taking off her new dress, she hung it in the wardrobe, the bitterness of its uselessness bringing tears to her eyes. She fought against them, drawing the curtains and switching on the light to make the room more cheerful. Then she had a hot bath and climbed into the double bed, trying not to notice how large it was. She took up the new novel she had brought home from the County Library on Wednesday. She tried to concentrate, but every now and again her eyes went to the empty pillow where Dick's head should be lying. She thought:

'Does he really love me? Has he ever really loved me? Did he marry me because he was used to me and I seemed safe and familiar after Anthea? after poor Mercia's death? Did he just want me as the right mother for little Mercia?'

She knew her thoughts were morbid and unreasonable. She and Dick had been passionate lovers, and until now she had never once doubted that he loved her as much as she loved him. Or if not in quite the same utterly devoted way in which she had loved him all her life, at least with complete sincerity and with all his physical being.

She remembered Adam's words, telling her not to make mountains out of molehills. Dick was not going to Cannes alone with Carol...his letter said he didn't really *want* to go. But it was strange that he should write—Dick who never put pen to paper unless he had to. His usual method of contact was by telephone. Writing almost made it look as if he were afraid to 'talk it over'—afraid she would make a fuss, try to stop him going.

'Perhaps I would have done!' Tamily told herself honestly. She had been stupid enough to show her jealousy of Carol last weekend. Dick would be quite justified in expecting her to go on being nasty.

'Maybe I put the idea of his being unfaithful into his head,' was Tamily's next unhappy thought. 'When he comes back I'll treat it all as perfectly natural, as if I understand.'

But try as she would she could not understand what was going wrong between them. She only knew that she would never have gone abroad with some man, no matter how important the business deal; no matter how much money was at stake. She wouldn't have wanted to go without Dick and Dick would surely have been against any such idea.

Suddenly she found herself wondering if this was true. Dick was never jealous. He had never had cause to be, for she had loved him faithfully since she was a small child and with a woman's complete passionate giving since they had grown up. Maybe he was too sure of her! In some books she read, men got bored with girls for whom they had not had to put up a chase. Maybe she should make Dick a little jealous—perhaps let him think she was attracted to Adam....

She closed her eyes, not liking the

thought of such shallow deceits. It ought not to be necessary. Surely part of love was complete faith and trust? And Dick would know that she wasn't really attracted to Adam.

She lay quietly, conjuring up Adam's face and strong square body. She recalled the comfortable feeling of security when she had wept on his shoulder this evening. Probably Adam had no idea of it, but he was the only man beside Dick in whose arms she had been. Of course, it had been a completely innocent embrace, but suppose that it were not—would she have minded if Adam had kissed her? Held her more tightly? Wanted her?

She was a little ashamed of such thoughts, but her lack of certainty puzzled her and would not let her drop the subject. She ought, surely, to feel repelled by the proximity of any man other than Dick? Yet Adam did not repel her. She had felt safe and warm and comforted. She had enjoyed that moment. It made her feel better.

She thought suddenly of his eyes— beautiful eyes, really. The tragedy of his approaching blindness swept all thought of herself from her mind. It was terrible and frightening to think of what lay in store for him. How must he feel, alone at night—on his own admission afraid? He needed someone beside him to comfort and sustain him. Her own loneliness was nothing compared with his.

Her pity leaped the short distance between them, and in her mind she stood beside his bed, a silent ghost whispering soft words of comfort to him. In her imagination, he held out his arms to her and she felt his need with a physical pang that caused her to bend over him and cradle his head against her bosom.

With a sense of shock she shook herself out of her imagination. This was wrong—in every way it was wrong. The last thing Adam wanted was pity—and the kindest thing she could do for him was to stay his friend. She must not use him—either for her own consolation, nor for the shady necessity of making Dick jealous.

She wondered whether she would feel embarrassed meeting him tomorrow. It was almost as if her thoughts had changed their relationship—destroyed its innocence.

But Adam, when he arrived at the house in the afternoon of the following day, was his usual self, and after the first few moments of shyness Tamily felt herself relax and soon began to talk to him unselfconsciously.

The picnic was fun. Mercia was as good as gold and ran about the woods picking bluebells in her hot sticky little hands and making tiny moss gardens under the trees.

'You obviously have a good effect on her!' Tamily told Adam as she spread out the picnic tea between them. 'She recognizes the voice of authority!'

With Dick the child always became over-excited and any outing with him ended inevitably in tears. Tamily thought now:

'It's Adam—he has a quiet, soothing effect, even on me.'

She ought to have been depressed and miserable today, knowing Dick was abroad with the Holmers; knowing she wouldn't see him now until next weekend. But she was enjoying the afternoon as much as little Mercia and was happy that Adam seemed to be as happy as they were. Dick was always so full of restless energy—to be with him was exciting, but always a little bit of a strain. He would become easily impatient if she were unable to keep up with him, treating her as he always had done, as if she were another boy.

Memories of their shared childhood flooded through her mind as she lay on her back looking up into the leafy branches of the tree above her.

'Come on, Tam! If I can climb it, you can.'

How many Easter holidays had they spent at the tops of trees, finding eggs for Dick's collection!

In a way their life together was still the same. Dick, anxious to get off to the village:

'Buck up, Tam! What on earth are you doing up there?'

He seemed not to realize that it took time to brush one's hair, touch up one's make-up, satisfy every woman's desire to look a little more attractive if she were going out with the man she loved.

Adam treated her very differently; as if she were fragile, almost as if she were a princess. It was strangely satisfying to be helped over stiles, even if you could manage them quite well alone! she thought. It was nice, too, to be lying like this quietly, without the need to talk. Had Dick been here he would have wanted to rush off to explore the woods or build a camp fire; or, if he were bored, which he possibly would be, make tracks for home where he could find something positive to do.

'I'm getting lazy in my old age!' Tam thought. Just lately she had had no energy for anything and seemed permanently on the point of falling asleep.

She sat up suddenly, her eyes wide with the thought that had darted across her mind. Her heart quickened its beat, and then, as she thought back, she knew that her guess was right—she was going to have a baby. It explained everything: the missed dates, the fatigue, the strange mixture of hunger and biliousness, the irritability and emotionalism. Now that she considered it, it was so obvious that she wondered how she had gone on so long without realizing it before.

She lay back, her hands behind her head, her eyes shut. She was very happy. Somewhere deep inside her she had been longing for a child—Dick's baby. They'd talked it over several times and she had agreed with Dick it would be better to wait...but she hadn't really wanted to wait. Mercia was growing up fast and it would be good for her to have a brother or sister; to have to learn to share and not to be the only pebble on the beach.

Her eyes opened again. Would Dick be pleased? Would he mind? She hoped desperately that he would be glad—as she was glad. There was no need to tell him yet—not until she had seen the doctor and made quite sure.

'Penny for them, Tamily!' Adam said quietly beside her. She hadn't realized that he had been lying on his side, watching her face.

She smiled, and for a moment the colour came into her cheeks. Then she said softly:

'All right, I'll tell you. But you must promise me not to tell a soul. The way I promised to keep *your* secret?'

He nodded.

'I was thinking about the baby I think I'm going to have. I'm not sure. But almost. Isn't it stupid of me...I've only just realized it.'

He swung round on his back quickly, to hide his expression from her. Her announcement was so unexpected he wasn't sure of his reactions. He was sure only of a great surging wave of jealousy. Now Allenton had everything—Tamily and her child. Lucky, lucky devil!

'You're happy about it?' he asked,

knowing from her voice that she was. 'Then I'm very happy for you. Does...doesn't Dick know?'

She shook her head, suddenly shy.

'Not yet. I'll tell him when I'm quite sure. I shouldn't really have told you, should I? But I just had to share my knowledge with someone.'

She suddenly thought how odd it was that she *could* tell Adam. Then, on reflection, it did not seem too strange. He was essentially a countryman—the cycle of birth, life and death were as natural to him, a farm bailiff, as to her. Only last spring she and Dick had helped him when one of the cows had difficulty calving and she had marvelled then at the gentle understanding of his hands as they managed the mother; had seen the quiet pleasure on his face when the struggling, leggy little calf had been born into his hands.

He said:

'I hope my sight will be spared long enough for me to see your child.'

Tamily was touched, unaware of the love that had prompted that cry from his heart; feeling only its simple sincerity.

'You must be godfather, Adam. That's a wonderful plan. Would you? I'm sure

Dick would like it, too. If it's a boy one of his names could be Adam.'

Adam got swiftly to his feet. There was too much dangerous sentiment in the conversation. In a moment he would break down and tell her that he loved her, desperately and more every moment; that his vow to subdue such feelings was getting harder with each time he saw her; that he'd give all the rest of his life to know that it was his child she carried and not Dick Allenton's.

'Come! Time to go home. I really must get back and do some work. Lord Allention will be giving me the sack if I don't pull up my socks. Where's that scamp Mercia?'

But he was not to escape so easily. With friendly innocence, Tamily linked her arm through his as they walked slowly home, her soft, sweet voice mingling with Mercia's higher-pitched tones. It was a moment of acute pathos—to be so close and yet so utterly removed from the vital core of her life.

7

Dick lay on his bed in the Carlton at Cannes, smoking a last cigarette before he went next door to collect Carol. He felt a lazy content and at the same time a tingling excitement.

The last few hours had been incredibly stimulating. First the drive to London Airport with Carol; then the lunchtime flight to Nice in the Comet. There had been a moment of embarrassment for Dick at the airport when Carol had handed him their tickets and an envelope full of money. He had hated taking them from her and yet it was *her* party....

Carol was obviously used to travelling luxuriously. A hired Fiat awaited them at Nice, in which Dick drove her to Cannes. At the Carlton adjoining rooms with private bathrooms were booked for them.

Carol had unpacked and come through into his room with iced champagne. There had been quite a party—ending in Dick's bed. Away from familiar surroundings, from Tamily and home, Dick had been less bothered by feelings of guilt and, as Carol had put it, it had been quite a session.

In a few moments they were going downstairs to dinner, then on to the casino in Cannes to play chemin de fer. He was excited and yet could not quite forget the two barbs to his pleasure: that he was cheating Tam and that Carol was paying for everything.

He sighed and stood up, going through the communicating door into Carol's room. It was filled with the smell of the scent she used—Guerlain's 'Shalimar'. The bedroom was gloriously untidy, strewn with her flimsy underclothes and make-up. It was very feminine—utterly unlike the room he shared with Tam at home. Their bedroom held no mystery, for it contained mostly his belongings—pictures of his old school, and Oxford University; his fishing-rod was propped up in one corner, and there were several photographs round it of school teams of which he was usually captain. Tamily had put them up there. She had kept them all since their childhood and refused stubbornly to put them away in a drawer, saying they were almost more a part of her life than his.

He walked across to the dressing-table where Carol was slipping slim coils of bracelets round her sun-browned arms. She looked unbelievably attractive in a new short evening dress. It was pleated silk, aquamarine coloured, the thousands of pleats moulded into the perfect shape of her figure.

Tonight her fair hair was brushed up and swathed into a bouffant style that was vaguely Grecian. She looked sleek, chic. She smiled up at Dick provocatively through long dark lashes.

'Hi!'

'Hi!' He kissed the nape of her neck.

She fitted a cigarette into the long amber holder he had bought for her at the airport. He had not wanted all the giving to be on her side. If only he could forget for a while! He consoled himself momentarily, remembering that it was really 'Dollar Dan' who was paying for this trip.

'My God, I'm weak!' Dick thought with sudden shame. 'I can't be near Carol without giving way to temptation.'

She watched him speculatively in the mirror, seeing the slight frown on his forehead. She guessed he was probably thinking of home and that dull little wife of his. Suddenly she hated Tamily; hated the idea of Dick belonging to anyone else but herself.

'Watch it, Carol!' she told herself sharply. 'Next thing you'll be in love with the guy!'

He looked older and extremely handsome in a dark blue lounge suit and white Italian silk tie. Very un-American—and dangerously attractive. Love wasn't part of her plan—she just wanted a good time. But Dick's 'hard-to-get' angle had roused something more in her than she had bargained for. Now she wanted to possess him completely—possess the part that still belonged to his wife.

'Love me just a little?' she asked huskily.

Dick blinked and stared down into those strange eyes.

'Mad about you!' he replied evasively. He couldn't talk of love—even in fun. He didn't love her...he just wanted her— couldn't seem to have too much of her.

They went down in the lift to the ground floor, left their keys at reception and strolled into the brilliantly lighted restaurant for dinner. The Carlton was full at this time of the year. An obsequious waiter showed them to a table by the huge glass windows overlooking the palm trees on the front. The sea was bright and dazzling in the summer sun.

They sat down, Dick feeling a quick elation. He'd noticed how all the other men in the room had turned to watch Carol as she walked to their table. They envied him. The thought gave him a thrill of possession—a possession to which he knew he had no right. But now he didn't care.

They lingered over a perfect meal. First, caviare followed by Steak Diane and then Crêpe Suzette. They watched with lazy satisfaction the waiter making the pancakes in his copper pan over the flames on his trolley. He poured in the brandy and orange curaçao; sifted in the sugar. He ignited it all. Blue flames leaped upwards. Then he turned the sizzling pancake which gave off a delicious odour; rolled it and put it on the plate with the reverence of a high priest.

The meal ended with a perfect Bresse Bleu cheese, coffee and cognac. Carol insisted Dick smoke a cigar, and he leaned back in his chair, momentarily relaxed and full of contentment. But before long he remembered that Carol, not he, would be paying for this meal, as for everything else, and his pleasure in it vanished.

Sensing his change of mood, Carol said:

'It's nearly ten o'clock, darling. What say we make tracks for the casino?'

The moon was silvering the deep blue waters of the Mediterranean as they walked from the hotel across to the casino. Already the Salle de Jeux was full. It was a cosmopolitan crowd. Men and women from all nationalities herded around the roulette tables, played chemin de fer or trente-et-quarante or lounged on stools at the long bar. Some were counting their winning chips; one or two looked depressed, as if they had lost heavily.

'I'm only interested in chemmy!' Carol announced.

'I'll come and watch you play,' Dick said.

'Nonsense!' Before he could stop her Carol slipped a roll of fifty New Franc notes into his hand.

'Here's a hundred pounds. Start with that and I'll do the same. If you lose it there's plenty more.'

Dick felt shaken. Although his family was rich, he had never seen money treated so carelessly. He protested at once, trying to hand the money back.

'I can't borrow from you, Carol. I don't know when I could pay it back.'

She cut him short, squeezing his fingers.

'It's not a loan, honey. Besides, on this trip what is mine is yours. Take it—to please me.'

Again, he protested, but Carol walked off, ignoring him. He paused for a moment, staring down at the notes. Then he went to change them into plaques. He liked the feel of the smooth bone counters—somehow they no longer represented the money given him by Carol....

He felt a quickening of his heart-beats as he heard the voices of the croupiers from the various roulette tables.

'*Faites vos jeux...*'

'*Rien ne vas plus...*'

From the Salle Privée came other exciting voices:

'*Mille francs à la banque. Messieurs, Mesdames...mille francs...qui fait le banque?*'

A hundred-pound bank—too big for Dick. The people sitting at the table also seemed to find it too high. Nobody spoke.

148

The croupier looked at Dick. Then Carol came up behind him.

'*Messieurs, Mesdames, mille francs à la banque!*'

Coolly, carelessly, smiling, Carol moved forward.

'*Banquo!*' she said with her strong American accent. She put a couple of plaques on the table.

The croupier smiled.

'*Banquo debout...seule!*'

The banker, a middle-aged Frenchman, flipped two cards out of the shoe toward the croupier, who handed them to Carol. Everyone was watching her now. Dick held his breath. Only the banker who stood to lose looked into space, pretending a bored disinterest.

Dick looked over Carol's shoulder. She had a three and a two. Carol never stood on five when the nearest to nine would sin. She said quietly:

'*Carte,* please!'

The banker came alive and turned his own cards over. He had a four and a three. Dick gave Carol an anxious glance. She would have to be lucky to beat a seven.

The Frenchman gave Carol a card and

tapped his own. He was standing on seven. Suddenly a gasp went up from the table as Carol turned over her card; Dick felt a thrill of pleasure—she had drawn another three. She put the cards down on the table, saying:

'*Huite!*'

The Frenchman shrugged. The croupier picked up a thousand New Francs worth of chips and handed them to Carol. Smiling, she whispered to Dick.

'See? You brought me luck, honey!'

A woman got up from the table. A footman beckoned Carol to the empty place. She sat down, looking cool, lovely and poised.

Dick had to wait a few moments for a place. He found one eventually at the other side of the salon. Here the stakes were slightly lower, but not much. The whole atmosphere breathed money, except for the obviously impecunious people who never actually played the games but strolled around, placing occasional bets on a running bank.

He sat back, watching, waiting for his shoe to come round to him. He was *Numero Sept*. He hoped it would be lucky. He wanted more than anything in the world to win so that he could pay Carol back.

He was sitting between a fat, bald-headed man in a check suit, with a strong Yankee accent, and a dark-haired girl in a pink linen dress. It was cut low to the waist at the back, high in front. She was wearing a lot of silver bracelets and a medallion on a long silver chain. She swung it to and fro and looked sideways at Dick.

Dick smiled at her, liking her face. He was used to women staring at him and always knew when a woman found him attractive. She smiled back.

Opposite him, a mature Indian woman in a fabulous purple and gold sari was playing beside her husband who wore gold-rimmed glasses. The man watched the play without moving a muscle of his dark face. Next to this couple sat a young fair-haired Englishman wearing a Guards tie. He was losing heavily and his cheeks were pale, his forehead glistening with sweat.

'He can't afford to lose!' Dick sensed. 'Any more than I could if Carol hadn't financed me.'

He felt a sudden savage desire to win.

The American sitting next to him now had the shoe. He began with two hundred and fifty New Francs. Dick knew it was more than he should gamble, but he tapped the table.

'Banquo—à la main!' said the croupier.

Dick picked up his cards. Damn! A couple of court cards. These were valueless.

'Carte! he said impatiently.

The American turned his over.

'Huite!' said the croupier, and swept away Dick's plaques.

A bad beginning, Dick thought nervously. In one minute he had lost a quarter of his money.

It was fatal to call suivi if you were short of money. To double at this stage was to risk five hundred francs. But Dick heard his voice call out the French word almost aggressively:

'Suivi!'

'Le banquo est suivi!' said the croupier in his bored, cold voice. He pushed two cards toward Dick.

Dick was sweating now. He picked up the cards. He had drawn a six and a valueless court card. he said:

'No card!'

The banker turned over his and the croupier's mechanical voice droned:

'Neuf à la banque!'

Nine! Luck was against him. Dick's lower lip pursed with disgust. But he managed somehow to look indifferent, too proud to show what the loss meant to him.

He did not *suivi* again. The dark girl beside him took the cards and won. 'Luck of the game!' Dick thought ruefully. Probably if he *had* called *suivi* he would have lost. The girl said softly:

'I'm sorry you had no luck.'

'Glad *you* had it!' he returned smoothly, and smiled into the friendly eyes. He felt a little better. Then his attention went back to the table.

During the rest of the shoe he had a mixture of good and bad luck. He finished with only twenty left from the hundred pounds Carol had lent him. Carol came over and laid a hand on his arm.

'Any luck?' she asked.

'Not too bad!' he said quickly. He still hoped to make it back.

Carol smiled at him.

'I've had fantastic luck—made six hundred dollars since I last saw you.'

Dick congratulated her. He said:

'Everything is drawn to you—men,

money and luck...'

'I'll settle for one of the three—men!' Carol said provocatively. 'Want to pack it in for tonight and go back to the hotel?'

He could not ignore the subtle flattery or the invitation in her eyes. His gaze travelled over her suntanned throat and satin-smooth arms. There wasn't a woman in the room to touch her, but, all the same, he wasn't ready to go—not yet.

'I'd like to have another go—run one good bank!' he said.

A man's voice droned above the hum and buzz of conversation:

'*Replenez vos places à table Numero Trois...*'

'That's for me,' said Carol. 'So long, honey. *Bon chance!*'

Back in his seat, Dick was asked to cut the pack of cards. Then the croupier re-stacked the five packs neatly in the shoe. The game began.

Halfway through the shoe Dick regained a few pounds. Then he ran a bank three times and at last piled a hundred pounds worth of chips in front of him. Now he felt better. He should quit now, but it occurred to him to try his luck a little longer. If he could make another hundred he could meet some of the hotel bills—buy Carol an expensive present....

The American next to him started a bank of twenty-five pounds. Dick lost and fell back on the old dangerous habit of calling *suivi* to a running bank. He lost his own bank and a *banquo* of the Indian lady opposite him. There was nothing more to lose.

He stood up, giving the rest of the players a hard, bright smile:

'See you later. Must go and change a cheque.'

But the desire to gamble had gone. He walked to the bar and, perching on a stool, sipped a whisky and soda. He suddenly loathed himself. He had been prepared to gamble Carol's money away, but he wasn't prepared to gamble his own.

But that was because it wasn't really his—it belonged also to Tamily—to the house and farm and the future.

As Carol came up to him, he said dejectedly:

'I'm afraid I've lost the lot, Carol. I feel an absolute heel. I will pay you back, though.'

Carol looked at his white face speculatively.

'See here, Dick, that was *not* a loan. I've won three times that amount tonight. Let's say you gambled away some of my winnings—that wasn't *my* money. It means merely that I won two hundred and not three. Forget it!'

But he still felt guilty. They walked back to the hotel in silence. Dick's thoughts were with Tamily, as he wondered once again how he could be cheating her like this. As if sensing his mood, Carol shivered and tucked her arm through his.

'We'll have a nightcap in my room, huh?' she asked.

He knew that he was far too weak ever to think of refusing.

It was nearly mid-morning when they breakfasted on the balcony outside Carol's room. The sun burned down on them and this morning Dick's good humour had returned. He felt full of energy and excitement at the prospect of the day ahead.

They swam before lunch and then made their way in beach clothes into Monte Carlo. After lunch Carol insisted they went round the shops. She bought many things: scarves, items of jewellery, perfume and a cocktail dress.

Shopping with Carol was an intriguing business for Dick. He had never been with a woman who spent so much money so carelessly, indulging every whim. Yet he could understand why she enjoyed giving herself these lovely things—whatever she tried on she looked beautiful in it. At last she turned to Dick and said laughing:

'Now I think we'd better go and win some more money to spend!'

They went in to the casino and played in the 'kitchen'. This time it was not only Carol whose luck held. Dick won again and again. At the end of the afternoon session he had a little over three hundred pounds. He was bursting with excitement.

'Look, Carol, here's your hundred back. And tonight, thank goodness, the party is on me.'

His success was like champagne. He drove Carol back to the hotel and this time she did not have to invite him to her room. He took her eagerly in his arms, saying gratefully:

'I'm having such fun, Carol—all thanks to you!'

Time passed all too quickly. That night they drove to Ville Franche, half an hour away along the coast. They dined in the

Château de Madrid, a restaurant on top of a cliff which they reached by lift. There was no dancing, so they lingered over the meal, lazily enjoying the good food and re-living their successes at the casino.

On Sunday they hired a launch to take them water ski-ing. It was Dick's first attempt and he took a number of duckings; but Carol was an expert and stirred Dick's admiration as she skimmed across the water in a minute white bikini, like a perfectly bronzed statue.

Later in the morning they drove to old Eze and lunched in a restaurant called Le Chevre d'Or. Here they ate a magnificent dish of bouillabaisse, looking down to the sea a thousand feet below. They bathed later in the outdoor swimming pool and lazed on the terrace where they had tea. Afterwards they drove back to Cannes for a last night at the casino.

Dick had only a few pounds left. Since winning at Monte Carlo he had paid for everything. Now, counting his francs, he was appalled to realize how much money he had run through in nothing more than luxury living. But he refused to regret it. Tonight he would win again, enough to pay the hotel bill and take Tamily home a magnificent present.

So far he had not bought her anything. He consoled himself that there would be plenty of opportunity and choice at the airport tomorrow morning. He'd wait and see how lavish a gift he could afford.

But, because he wanted so badly to win, luck was against him. Carol, too, dropped a hundred pounds before she began once more to win. During the evening she gave Dick a handful of plaques.

'Come on, honey! These are lucky ones. You'll win with them.'

Again, hating the thought of her subsidizing him, he tried to decline. But, laughing, Carol walked back to her table, leaving the chips in his hands. Recklessly, he plunged back into the game.

Again and again the cards went against him. Once more, Carol came over and dropped a handful of chips in front of him. But even though he won once or twice he always lost far more than he won.

At midnight he had nothing left. Carol tried to cheer him, showing him her handbag stuffed with notes. It seemed not to worry her in the least that he had run through three hundred pounds.

'Forget it! Please, honey?'

But the night, the holiday, everything had suddenly become stale and unpalatable. His conscience was back, troubling him more than ever. What a weak silly fool he was! If he had kept away from the tables he could have avoided this. Now there was not time to play again—to win enough to pay Carol back, even if his luck were to return.

Tomorrow he would be going home—back to the office, and, at the weekend, back to Tamily. And he hadn't enough money even to buy her some decent perfume.

Feeling sick and shaken, he drove Carol back to the hotel. He would have slept alone that night had he been able, but Carol was persistent and refused to listen to his pleas that they both needed a good night's rest.

'The more I have of you, the more I want!' she whispered to him hungrily. 'You're like a drug to me, darling. It isn't going to be easy to get you out of my system. Dick, you do love me, don't you? Just a little, tiny bit?'

He hadn't the heart to tell her he did not love her at all, nor, at this moment, even desire her beautiful body. He wished frantically that he had never come; never given way to temptation; never been so revoltingly weak as to be unfaithful to poor Tamily.

He saw himself suddenly as his wife would see him—little better than a gigolo, paid for and kept by Carol. How could he go home to her and admit that this was the kind of man she had married?

Most of all, he despised himself for the thought that had he won at chcmin dc fcr tonight he might not be feeling like this.

'Chin up, honey! It's just the luck of the draw. Don't let it get you down!'

Carol's voice beat against his thoughts. He took her in his arms, trying to feel grateful, trying to recapture the excitement, the champagne-like atmosphere of the morning.

But it was gone—and he knew it would never come back again.

8

On Monday evening Dick telephoned to his wife to tell her he was back in the flat once more. He had resolved not to lie to her any more than was necessary. The truth, of course, was quite out of the question. Tamily would never understand how he could have spent a long weekend with another woman even although it had taught him a severe lesson.

Never again, he told himself throughout the day. Even the good time with Carol had been spoilt by his guilty conscience, and now the knowledge that he had allowed her to spend so much money seemed even worse in retrospect. Carol did not expect him to pay it back—she had said so and meant it. But he would have felt better if he could have done so. Now he was under an obligation which made things very awkward as he had decided not to see her again.

The first lie came when Tamily asked after Carol's father. With a shock Dick remembered that Mr Holmer was supposed to have been with them in Cannes. He was forced to improvise news of the man he hadn't seen in over a week. He was not a good liar and he was afraid Tamily might suspect something from his rambling account of their activities. When she suddenly said, 'Nothing's wrong, is it, Dick?' he was badly shaken.

He said hurriedly: 'I'm afraid I lost a bit of money gambling at the casino. I—I'm sorry, Tam!'

She made no complaint—just replied:

'You can tell me about it at the weekend. Don't worry about it, Dick. I'm glad you are back.'

'Tammy, I love you!' he said impulsively. He heard across the wires her intake of breath, then her voice saying softly:

'And I love you, darling! That's all that matters, isn't it? I've hated this weekend, knowing all the time that you were such miles away; knowing I couldn't phone you. I wish it was Friday now.'

'I'll come down Friday immediately after I leave the office!' he promised. 'Don't fix anything up, Tam. We'll have a long restful weekend, just the two of us.'

Putting down the phone, he realized

that this was just what he ought not to be planning. Tam would ask endless questions he would, somehow, have to answer. She would look at him with that direct wide-eyed gaze of hers and sooner or later she would guess he was hiding something from her.

He wished like hell that he could 'own up'—get it all off his chest and his conscience, the way he had as a boy. Easy when one was young—one took the punishment and the misdeed was forgotten. But Tam simply wouldn't understand or forgive—he wasn't even sure he understood himself!

He lay on his bed, trying to puzzle out his behaviour. The attraction Carol had for him was purely physical and easy enough to understand. What seemed so improbable was that he had agreed to go away with her, and that he had agreed to let her finance the trip. A momentary lapse, such as had occurred in the flat the previous week—that was weak but excusable. The deliberate planning of their holiday in Cannes—it was crazy!

But no more crazy than gambling away several hundred pounds of Carol's money! God, how he wished he could repay it!

He could only do so by depleting their farm savings account—undoing years of hard saving. It wasn't even morally *his* money. Tam had been managing on far less than she need in order to help him save. She never bought clothes or things for the house unless they were absolutely necessary.

The more Dick reflected, the meaner he felt. It was a relief when the phone rang, even although it was Carol. Talk might stop him thinking and worrying. But the relief was only momentary. Carol said:

'Dad's downstairs drinking with some cronies. I'm so bored, honey. Can I come round and see you?'

'No!' His refusal was so instantaneous and heart-felt that he felt forced to soften it. He said more gently:

'I meant what I said on the plane this morning, Carol. We can't keep on betraying Tam. It's over now—finished.'

When she spoke her voice was tinged with a new hardness.

'Easy come, easy go, eh, Dick? Take what's offered and light out!'

'Carol, please don't feel bitter about it. It would all be quite different if I weren't married. I can't have a prolonged love affair and you know it. Tamily would find out and we've no right to hurt her.'

'But it's okay to hurt me?'

'Carol! You aren't really *hurt*—not the way Tamily would be. You knew from the beginning I wasn't in love with you. You aren't in love with me, either.'

'No? Maybe I should be too proud to admit this, but I am in love with you. Now what can you do about that?'

Dick drew in his breath.

'You just think you are, Carol. The fact that I'm not available and your being used to having what you want, probably lends me a false desirability. Please don't make things complicated.'

'Damn it, they are complicated!' Carol was almost shouting. 'You know how I feel—' She broke off, as if realizing that this was getting her nowhere. More quietly, she said:

'Look, couldn't I at least come around so's we can talk this over? I promise not to misbehave.'

'No, Carol. Apart from anything else, it's nearly midnight and I've got to be at the office tomorrow. I must get some sleep.'

'Okay! Tomorrow, then. Lunch with me.'

'No, Carol! If it makes you feel any happier to know it, I daren't! I'm so blasted weak. I don't want to get any deeper involved. Honestly, I'm terribly grateful and I'll never forget you—never. I had a marvellous time and I think you're a marvellous person. But it's best if we both forget each other.'

'Sounds awfuly corny to me, honey. Did you get that out of a book?'

'Carol, please!'

'And what do I say to Dad? Thanks for the trip, Dad, but it's all off—he's bored with me!'

'Carol, don't! It isn't like that. I ought never to have gone with you and you know it. I'm no good to you or to my wife. But I must at least try, for Tamily's sake, to do what's right.'

'A fine time for new resolutions—after the ball is over!'

'I know that. I know I should never have gone at all. I'm truly sorry, Carol.'

'You're a coward!' Carol said flatly. 'You were in the casino and now it's the same.'

Dick flushed.

'You've every right to call me names, Carol, but I'm not *afraid*. I wish to God I had been afraid—then I wouldn't have gambled so much of your money away.'

'How about that!' Carol said, her voice suddenly changing and becoming almost teasing. 'Not afraid to blue two or three hundred pounds, but afraid to see me again.'

Dick ground out his cigarette in a nearby ashtray and said angrily:

'Please try to understand, Carol. I'm not afraid to see you but I am afraid to hurt Tammy—she has never done a harmful thing to anyone in the whole of her life. You don't know her the way I do. She's simple and good and sweet—not like us!'

'Like us!' Carol repeated the words dreamily. 'We're two of a kind. That's what I've been trying to tell you, honey. It's why we hit it off so well in bed, too. We understand each other.'

'It's no good, Carol. I hate to say this, but I'm not in love with you. I'm in love with Tamily.'

'Tell that to your grandmother!' Carol said rudely. 'What man "in love",' she stressed the words scornfully, 'goes off

168

for three days and nights with another woman!'

'Probably dozens—when the other woman is as attractive as you are, Carol. I expect there are plenty more like me who are too weak to say no to temptation. But that's sex, Carol, not love—and you know it!'

'What ever it is, I want you!' Carol said quietly. 'Nor do I ever give up what I want easily. Good night, darling. Sleep tight. I'll be seeing you.'

She rang off before he could speak again. He got back into bed and lit another cigarette. Somehow Carol's last words had sounded like a threat! Not that she would do anything—but...well, hell hath no fury like a woman scorned. She could hurt him if she wanted to.

But she wouldn't—she couldn't! Dick tried to reassure himself. He'd just keep out of her way—hope she'd see that it was really all over and go off somewhere else to have a good time.

He tried to sleep—but he was haunted first by Carol's face and then by Tamily's. His mind went back to the past when he had been in other scrapes. Tammy had helped him out of those. This time he couldn't go to her for help. Would it be best to confess everything? Best for him—but not for Tammy. She had never done a nasty thing in her life. He couldn't expect her to understand.

He twisted and turned and tried not to think about tomorrow. He hoped Carol would not try to contact him at the office. Maybe he *should* lunch with her—nothing could happen at lunch in a crowded restaurant. He might be able to talk her into understanding that their affair must end—had ended.

But it was Carol's father who telephoned him next morning; Carol's father who insisted they should have a meal together.

The older man greeted Dick in a friendly enough manner. Dick wondered just how much he knew about their weekend in Cannes. Harry Holmer did not leave him long in doubt.

'See here, young man,' he said as soon as they were seated in the comparative privacy of their table. 'I like you and I'm not here to make things difficult for you. The fact is, I have to talk to you about Carol.'

He took a long drink of beer and eyed Dick over the rim of his glass.

'She's fallen for you in a big way,' he

went on. 'Told me this morning she was heart-broken because you wanted to end your—er—friendship.'

'I'm very sorry!' Dick said lamely. 'But Carol knew all along I was married—that our friendship couldn't come to anything!'

'I know, I know! You've been perfectly honest with her and I am not criticizing you. No one is to blame for this, although I'll grant that my baby is a very headstrong little girl. She told me herself she sure did not mean to fall in love. But there it is. The question now is what are we going to do about it.'

Dick looked at his companion uncomprehendingly.

'What *can* I do about it? The best thing is for me to stop seeing her. She'll soon forget me.'

'That's not what I meant!' A little of the man's geniality had gone. His voice was a shade harder, more business-like. Now Dick could see how he had made his million—the hard, ruthless, astute business man was coming to the fore.

'It isn't a question of ending it, Dick. It is a matter of thinking of a way round existing difficulties so everyone is happy.'

'There is no way round,' Dick replied, puzzled and uneasy.

'There always is—if you can afford it. Now see here—just listen to me a moment without interrupting. I've met your wife—a charming girl and no doubt one who could make the average man perfectly happy. But you aren't average, Dick. You've got it in you to go places. You could get where I've got if you wanted it badly enough, boy. I started fifty years ago with exactly two dollars in my pocket; now, in American dollars, I'm a millionaire.'

'Yes, but—'

'Listen to me, boy. You've got a big advantage over me. You're well bred; you've had a first-class education and you're good-looking. Moreover, you could have me behind you. I'd be willing to back you up no matter what business you chose to take up. And you'd succeed, Dick. You'd be in my shoes before you were thirty! The whole world at your feet. And what is the only stumbling-block? I'll tell you—your wife. You need a woman who can stand up alongside you—travel, entertain—who knows her way around. My Carol could do all that. You couldn't choose a better wife.'

Dick could no longer contain himself. Outraged, he said:

'But I have a wife—a wife I'm in love with. Divorce is out of the question. Besides—'

'Why out of the question? Money can get you anything you want in this life, Dick. You don't have to worry about your wife. I'll see she has a very generous settlement—enough for her to live comfortably with the child for the rest of her life. I'll guarantee it even if she marries again and then it's certain she won't stay a alone for long. Rich, pretty divorcees don't have to wait for husbands. Why, she could marry that gamekeeper fellow your father employs—forget his name. They'd have money enough to stock the farm and run it independently of your father. Now, don't answer me in a hurry, Dick. Think about it.'

Dick was too shocked to reply. When he got his breath back some of his anger had evaporated. He was forced to realize that this man was not intentionally insulting him. All his life Harry D. Holmer had been made to pay for what he wanted. That he thought he could buy anything—even people—was, no doubt, due to the fact

173

that the kind of people he'd met *could* be bought. It was not his fault that he should think Dick, too, had no moral values; no ideals. On Dick's behaviour so far, Holmer had made a fair summing-up.

The waiter served the first course. As soon as he had gone Dick said gently:

'Please don't think I'm ungrateful for your suggestion. I know you mean it as a compliment—but the fact is, Mr Holmer, I don't need to consider it. However long I thought about it, the answer would always be no—for a variety of reasons.'

'Such as?'

'Well, they may not be reasons you'll understand. But I'll tell you them all the same. First, I love my wife. Second, even if I did not love her I would never willingly hurt her, because she loves me. Thirdly, although I grant your daughter is very, very attractive, I am not in the least in love with her. Lastly, and not necessarily least, I could not enjoy a penny of the money I might make, knowing that it was come by through your power rather than my own ability.'

Harry Holmer grunted.

'A very fine speech—but not altogether sincere towards the end. Pride is all very well, young man, but it has to be consistent. You were not too proud to accept my money while you were in France. Nor too proud to enjoy gambling it away.'

Dick's mouth tightened.

'Okay, so I didn't live up to my principles. Believe me, Mr Holmer, since I've been back I've been deeply regretting it. I felt lousy at the time and I've felt worse each time I've remembered I let Carol foot the bills. I'm in your debt to the tune of about four hundred pounds and, believe me, that rankles too. Enough, certainly, to know that I wouldn't like it to be four million pounds. I'll pay it back, Mr Holmer.'

To Dick's surprise the American chuckled.

'Okay, I like your spirit. But I don't want your money. I'm after my little girl's happiness—that's all I want. Name your own terms, Dick.'

'There aren't any "terms"!' Dick cried. 'Can't you understand? This time Carol can't have what she wants.'

For a moment silence hung heavily between them. Dick laid down his knife and fork, but Mr Holmer continued eating. Suddenly he looked up and said:

175

'If you'd not been married, boy? Would you have married Carol then?'

Dick shrugged.

'I can't answer that. I just don't know. I do know I wouldn't have married Carol for her money. I'd have to have been in love. I admire your daughter very much but... Well, what's the good of talking about it. Nothing on God's earth would make me leave Tam.'

'Well, at least that has cleared up a number of points!' the American said, his voice friendly again. 'Let's forget it now, shall we? Maybe Carol will decide to move on. We'll see. Tell me now, how was the trip? Wish I could have gone along....'

Dick relaxed, feeling as if he escaped from an invisible trap. He might have been less relieved if he had known what was at the back of Harry Holmer's mind. But he was hard at work in the office when Carol's father reported his findings to his daughter in their hotel suite.

'Can't talk him round, honey! He ain't to be bought like that South American boy of yours. If it's done at all it'll have to be at the other end.'

Carol's face was hard.

'Meaning?'

'If he won't leave his wife she'll have to leave him!'

Carol bit angrily at the knuckle of her hand.

'That's ridiculous. You saw her. She's crazy about him. You won't get a woman in love to give up her man for money!'

Harry Holmer puffed at his cigar, his face relaxed and unworried.

'That's exactly my point, honcy. She loves him. If she didn't it wouldn't be all so easy.'

Carol stamped her foot like a petulant child.

'Will you please explain what you're getting at?'

'Sure I will. It's like this, Carol. All my life I've studied human nature. It isn't very often people step out of line—give a certain set of circumstances and this is how they'll react. So—what happens when a loving wife discovers her husband has been unfaithful? If she happens to be a bit bored with him or not too much in love with him she'll probably make a big scene, forget about it and pay him back by being unfaithful herself. But if she loves him she'll never let him forget how much he has hurt her and then he'll walk out.'

Carol smiled understandingly.

'Could work. But there's no guarantee Dick would turn to me.'

'And why not—if you play your cards right? No more calling him up and making life difficult for him, honey. From now on you are his understanding, sympathetic *friend*. Who else would he turn to in time of trouble?'

Carol flung her arms round her father's neck in a rare gesture of affection.

'Pop, you're a marvel!' she said. 'A clever, clever daddy.'

She ruffled his hair and said thoughtfully:

'You've no scruples—about her?'

Harry Holmer shrugged.

'Why should I have scruples? She may be unhappy for a little while, but believe me, honey, a nice fat bank account can make the unhappiest woman smile again. That is unless she's blasé about money the way you are! I've spoilt you, baby, and that's for sure!'

Carol grinned.

'I still enjoy money!' she said softly. 'It's just that right now I badly want Dick Allenton, too. You like him, don't you, Dad?'

He pursed his lips.

'He has his faults. He might be more of a man if he'd come up the hard way, like me. His father knows it—that's why he has tightened up on the purse-strings now. But as a son-in-law Dick won't do too badly. I can manage him—and so could you. Moreover, baby—and this has weighed fairly heavily with me all along—young Dick will be Lord Allenton eventually and it tickles me to think of you with a title—old Dollar Dan's daughter a Lady. That'll make 'em sit up in the club at home.'

'You're a snob!' Carol said flatly, but there was no rancour in her voice. It did not matter what reasons her father had for helping her get what she wanted. It was enough that he was on her side.

9

The letter arrived Saturday morning by the first post. Dick was still lazing in bed, Tamily cooking the breakfast, when the long thin envelope dropped through the letter-box. Tamily went through into the hall and picked it up, noting with surprise that it was type-written and addressed to her.

She took it into the kitchen and put the bacon slices under the grill before she sat down at the table and opened it.

Dear Dick! it began. Tamily frowned and looked again at the envelope. Yes, it was addressed to her. She glanced at the end of the page and saw the signature, *Harry D. Holmer.* Was it a belated thank-you letter meant for them both? So far there had been no written thanks from the Holmers for their weekend stay at Lower Beeches.

She glanced at the grill and turned back to the letter.

I know you will have been worrying about

180

our lunchtime discussion last Tuesday and so I am hastening to write to tell you that you can forget all about it. Carol is slowly coming round to accepting the fact that you can't leave your wife to marry her...

Tamily gasped, her face chalk-white. She knew now that the letter was meant only for Dick, but she could not help herself. Knowing this much, she had to know more.

She is still pretty shaken, as she really had thought there was some hope while the pair of you were in Cannes. I think I made her understand that your sense of duty and obligation would never permit you to desert a wife who depended solely upon you. Given time, I think Carol will settle for keeping you as a very dear friend.

Please do not give another thought to the cost of the trip or the gambling losses. They are no more than a drop in the ocean to me and under no circumstances would I permit you to pay these few hundreds back. My little girl had a wonderful time and that's all the return I need.

My kindest regards to your wife and I look forward to lunching with you again next week

when we can discuss purely business affairs.
                                   Yours sincerely,
                                   Harry D. Holmer

P.S. Carol will not be making contact with you until she has herself under control. Then I know she will want to meet you again as a friend.

The bacon began to burn. Automatically Tamily removed it from under the grill and tipped it into the refuse-bin. With the same automatic actions she cut off the rind and put fresh slices on to cook.

Inside her a voice was screaming: 'No! No! No!'

At last her legs began to tremble so violently that she was forced to sit down. She covered her face with her hands. Thoughts began to take shape. Dick—last night—holding her in his arms...making love to her. Dick, swearing that it had been rather a dull weekened, relieved only by the excitement of gambling and even that had been spoilt by his heavy losses. Dick begging her to forgive him for wasting their years of saving when all the time...

'Tam, where's my break— Why, what's the matter, darling? Aren't you well?'

She drew back from his outstretched arm with a look of horror. Looking into her eyes, Dick was suddenly terrified. What had happened to her? Had she suddenly gone out of her mind?

Slowly her arm raised and she pointed to the letter lying on the kitchen table. Dick took a step forward, reaching out for it, his own face white now as he anticipated what he would read. As he picked up the single tell-tale sheet he guessed that last night's lies had been for nothing.

He finished reading it and, desperately angry and upset, he rounded on Tamily.

'You'd no right to read my mail—to open it...'

He stopped as she pushed the envelope towards him. There was no doubting what was written there—*Mrs* Richard Allenton. Not Richard Allenton, Esq., but *Mrs*. What can have possessed Harry Holmer to write such a letter—and to his home, too? Was it his secretary's mistake? If so it was an unforgivable one. The damage could never be undone.

'Tam, I'm sorry! Most of all I'm sorry that you should have learned the truth like this. I wanted to tell you—to beg you to try and forgive me. The only reason I didn't do so last night was because I was so afraid of hurting you. Tam...'

'You lied! You said Carol's father was with you. You said it was a *dull* weekend. You said you weren't in the least attracted to her. You said—'

'Stop it! I know I told lies—I had to. Don't you see, I had to tell them to stop you finding out.'

It was as if he hadn't spoken. She went on in her quiet, even voice as if she were calling out a shopping list:

'You said you loved me. Last night you told me you could never love any other woman but me. You—'

'And it was *true*. Tam, I do love you—I've never stopped loving you. Can't you try to understand? It's true, too, that I didn't really want to go in the first place. I was weak, I know that. But most of the while I was hating myself. Tamily, please don't look at me like that. Please try to understand.'

She was very quiet. Her face was without colour, her eyes enormous. He might have found it easier to deal with her if she had broken down and cried. But she was quite unapproachable, withdrawn—like a stranger.

'Go on then, Dick. Explain it to me. Explain how a man who loves his wife can plan a dirty weekend abroad with another woman. How a man who is happily married can let that other woman believe he would marry her if he hadn't got a devoted little wife at home whom duty forbade him to leave. Explain how a man can let another woman pay for his dirty weekend—pay his gambling debts and then, when he has taken all there is to take, go running home to his devoted little wife for a little bit more love-making. Is there some special thrill, Dick, in going to bed with two women alternately? Did it all seem so special last night because you'd learned some new tricks from *her?* Maybe you've got the right idea! Maybe I should go and sleep with Adam Bond and then I could show you a few things too.'

'Tamily!'

He raised his hand—not because he meant to strike her but to stop the terrible words that were pouring out of her. She flinched away from him, her cheeks flushed now, her eyes burning.

'Go on, then, and hit me! You can't hurt me any more than you have done already. I hate you—do you hear? *I hate you!*'

She ran out of the room. Dick supposed she had gone to their bedroom where no doubt she would lock the door against him. He did not follow her, for he guessed that anything he could say at this moment would be useless. From Mercia's bedroom came a wail:

'Mummy, I want to get *up!*'

Dick went to the child, lifting her out of bed and holding her close for a moment before he put her down on the floor. Her pretty innocent little face seemed like an added rebuke. She reminded him so much of his sister. How Mercia would have hated him! How he hated himself! Tamily might not realize it but he was suffering as deeply as she was right now.

'Where's Mummy? I'm hungry. I want to wear *that* dress!'

Her voice became petulant and demanding. Through his misery Dick was conscious of the child's imperious little demands.

'Tam was right—she is getting spoilt!' he thought. 'We ought to have a baby of our own. Mercia has been king of the castle too long!'

But it was a little late to be discovering this. This was scarcely the moment to think about additions to a family that was perilously near disintegration.

As he sat Mercia in her high chair and gave her something to eat he told himself not to take such a desperate view of the situation. Of course, Tamily had had a nasty shock—but she would get over it. She must get over it. Even if it took a long time she had to forgive him in the end. It wasn't possible that she would want a divorce?...

The possibility so appalled him that he left Mercia to her own devices and ran upstairs. Their bedroom door was ajar. The room was empty. Breathing deeply, Dick stood looking round. It wasn't possible that Tam had run away?—grown-up people didn't walk out of the house for good, leaving everything....

He walked over to the cupboard and checked Tamily's clothes. As far as he could remember nothing was missing. Her handbag lay on the dressing-table.

He went downstairs and, ignoring Mercia's screams from the kitchen, phoned the Manor. Jess answered.

'Is Tamily there?' Dick asked without preamble.

'At this time of the morning, Dick?

Whatever made you think she'd be here? Nothing is wrong, is it?'

He'd had enough of lies. He said quietly: 'We've had a bit of a row, Jess. Tam's disappeared. I thought she might have come up to you.'

'I'm sorry, Dick. She isn't here. Don't worry too much—she'll be back, I'm sure.'

'I'd better ring off—I can hardly hear for Mercia, who's screaming her head off in the kitchen.'

'I'll come down and take her off your hands just as soon as I've finished here,' Jess said. 'You can tell me about it then.'

Relieved by his mother-in-law's calm voice, Dick went back into the kitchen and tried to pacify Mercia. Although she usually made no bones about the fact that she preferred Dick, this morning, just to be awkward, she wanted her mother. Dick felt like smacking her—but refrained. Perhaps the child sensed the tension—children did.

He sat down, lit a cigarette and tried not to think.

★ ★ ★ ★

Down by the stream Tamily lay full

length in the long grass and tried to cry. Her heart ached so badly she felt instinctively that tears would ease the pain. But no tears came. The grass smelt hot and sweet. Soon it would be time for the second hay harvest. The first was already in, baled and stored away in the barn against the coming winter.

Her eyes followed a ladybird climbing a stalk. It's tiny scarlet black-spotted wings opened and closed as if it could not make up its mind to fly.

'Ladybird, ladybird, fly away home. Your house is on fire and your children all gone!'

She said the words she had learned in the nursery and touched the tiny insect with the tip of her finger. It flew off at once.

'Your children all gone!' Tamily whispered. Such a sad little song—sad as she was sad for something lost that could never come back. She thought for the first time of the child inside her, and wished with a savage desire that it was not there. She didn't want it now—not a miniature Dick to hurt and torment her; to betray and cheat her; to stamp on all her dreams and crumble them into dust.

She wondered suddenly if it was her fault—if somehow she had failed Dick. A book she had once read had said that if a husband was unfaithful it was often as not the wife's fault. At once her childhood inferiority complex returned. She had never felt that she was 'good enough' for Dick. As a young girl she had not dared to dream that one day Dick might fall in love with her. Even after Dick had proposed to her she had been afraid his parents might object. Tamily would not have blamed them. Their kindness to her did not alter the fact that she was the illegitimate daughter of their housekeeper; ordinary, dull, not even particularly pretty. Dick could laugh at her—telling her not to be a snob; not to feel that *she* was to blame because her father had run out on her mother; not to mind that she wasn't academically brilliant, clever or witty because he liked her as she was.

Had he been lying? Had he married her because he'd felt sorry for her? Because he had wanted little Mercia and known that Tamily wanted her, too? There were many reasons why he might have married her other than for love. She'd always known it and only felt utterly secure at moments of shared passion. Then she had felt in the deepest parts of her being that Dick, for the moment, anyway, was heart and soul her own.

She felt suddenly sick. Maybe she had been wrong about this, too. For all she knew, men might all behave as Dick did, tenderly, lovingly, after their passion had been satisfied. For all she knew, Dick might have seemed to the American girl just as completely hers.

The nausea became worse and the next moment Tamily was being very sick.

'Great Scot, *Tamily!* Are you all right? Here, take my handkerchief!'

Before she could say thank you she was sick again. This time Adam Bond held her head in cool, firm hands. When it was over he held her arms, looking anxiously into her white face and said:

'Feel strong enough to go home?'

Her whole body shuddered.

'I don't want to go home!'

'But you're shivering. You're not well!'

The kindness and anxiety in his voice was suddenly the key unlocking the tears. Now at last she could feel sorry for herself. She began to weep.

'Tamily, stop it! If you won't stop crying

191

for your own good, at least stop for mine. I can't stand to see you cry!'

His words had the desired effect. She wiped her eyes and sniffed into his handkerchief.

'I'm sorry, I'm sorry!' she said.

'If you won't go back to your own home then you must come to mine,' Adam said firmly. 'What you need is a good strong cup of tea laced with brandy.'

He helped her to her feet and they began to walk back to Adam's house. He did not ask any questions until she was sitting in his leather armchair, the half-empty teacup in her hands.

'Feeling better?'

She nodded.

'You don't look it. You ought to go home!'

'I can't, Adam. I can't!'

'Of course you can!' he said firmly. 'It's your home, Tamily, and no matter what has happened, that is where you should be. Home and safely tucked up in bed. Want to tell me what's wrong?'

In the ordinary way Tamily would never have confided in Adam. Her life with Dick was their private affair. But now, having been found quite accidentally by

Adam, she felt she owed him some kind of explanation. She said hesitantly: 'Dick and I...we had a quarrel. I...I don't want to go back.'

He was silent as he walked away from her and stared out of the window. He dared not stay near her; the longing to put his arms around her and kiss away that stricken look was almost more than he could bear. She looked for all the world like some animal imprisoned in a trap. The fact that she had quarrelled with Dick did not make him happy, even though it had brought her to his house for a little while—an unexpected gift from the gods. Just to have her sitting there—knowing she was in the same room, breathing the same air—was enough to make him happy. But he did not want his own happiness at the expense of hers. He said gently:

'Life is too short for quarrels, Tamily. Whatever has happened can't be irrevocable. Go back and make it up. Young Dick is probably worried to death at this moment. I think I ought to ring through and tell him you are here.'

She half rose from the chair.

'You're not to do that. I don't want

to see Dick. He might come here to fetch me!'

'Then let me ring your mother. If Dick gets in touch with her she'll be worried. Maybe you could go up to the Manor for a few days until you've both calmed down a little.'

Tamily drew a long breath of relief.

'That's a wonderful idea, Adam. I ought to have come to you in the first place—I'm sure there isn't a problem in the world you couldn't deal with.'

Adam smiled.

'I wish that were true! All the same, Tamily, don't decide in a hurry. The wider the rift, the more difficult it is to breach when you do want to do so. Running away from your problems isn't the best way to solve them, either. Sometimes it is better to face up to them.'

Tamily ran her hand through her hair nervously. What Adam said made sense. Sooner or later she would have to make up her mind to face Dick—decide about the future. She wasn't at all sure at this moment if she could bear to go on living with him. Certainly she could not bear him to touch her.

Suddenly she remembered Mercia. She

194

hoped Dick had been able to cope with the child.

'I ought to go back!' she said hesitantly.

Adam came across the room and laid a hand on her shoulder.

'I think so, too—' he began, when at that moment the door burst open and Dick flung into the room.

It was whilst he was waiting for Jess that the first suspicion came to him that Tamily might have gone to Adam Bond's house. He remembered with a sick feeling in the pit of his stomach her angry taunt: *'Maybe I should go and sleep with Adam Bond and then I could show you a few things...'*

At the same time Harry Holmer's words in the restaurant stirred his memory. *'...she could marry that gamekeeper fellow your father employs....'*

For the first time in his life Dick felt a searing jealousy. Since their schoolroom days he had been absolutely certain of Tamily's love for him—a love which had deepened as the years went by. Only once in her life had she looked at another man—a young Frenchman who had found her attractive. But even then Tamily had admitted she'd only wanted to make Dick jealous! He had never had cause to doubt her love—until now. Now he suddenly realized that other men could and did exist for her. Maybe she had not been unfaithful but the thought must have been there....

Jess's greeting added fuel to the flames. 'It's just possible she may have gone down to Adam's house. They have become good friends recently and...'

Dick rushed out of the house, leaving his mother-in-law staring anxiously after him.

He stood now in Adam's simple, unpretentious room, staring from Tamily's flushed face to the man's thoughtful one. Both looked surprised to see him. Finding Tamily here confirmed his fears. He said bitterly:

'To think I apologized to you for my behaviour. Why, you're no better than I am—and *I* begged *you* to forgive *me!*' He gave an angry glance at Tamily's bowed head. 'So you can't even look me in the face!' he shouted at her. 'As for you, Bond—I'll get you fired—'

'Dick!' Tamily's voice cut across his in anger. 'If you don't shut up I'll leave you—divorce you. And it won't be Adam who is fired. You father will kick *you* out!'

He had never heard her use that cold, hard voice before. He became a little less sure of himself.

'You were just waiting for me to give you an excuse for running to *him!*' he blustered, pointing an accusing finger at Adam. 'And all the time you pretended you were so deeply shocked and outraged by my behaviour. Well, all I can say—'

'Allenton, you'd better stop talking that way. You don't know what you are saying. Tamily did not come to me. I found her by the stream. She wasn't well, so I brought her back here and gave her a brandy. She was just about to come home when you turned up.'

Dick looked at the older man scornfully.

'You expect me to believe that?'

'You can believe it or not, as you choose,' Adam said calmly. 'It happens to be the truth. Moreover, I think you owe your wife an apology.'

Tamily suddenly burst into tears.

'I don't *want* an apology. I don't care what he believes. He can believe it's true if he wants. Maybe I am in love with you, Adam. Maybe I would rather be married to you than to a...a man like *him!*'

'Tamily!'

Adam's voice was pleading with her. But she was beyond caring now. The combination of shock and nausea and the general feeling of being unwell in early pregnancy was too much for her.

'Go away and leave me alone!' she shouted to Dick. 'Nobody asked you here. Tell him to go, Adam. I don't want to have to look at him. I hate him!'

Adam looked from one to the other unhappily. As Dick took a step towards his wife Adam intervened.

'I think you had better go,' he said quietly. 'She'll calm down in a little while.'

Dick looked at the man furiously.

'Don't you tell me how to manage my wife. You come home with me this minute, Tamily. Do you hear me?'

For one long moment she stared at him speechlessly. Then, her voice suddenly quiet, she said:

'You can't make me do anything I don't want to do, Dick. And you've no right—*no right at all*—to dictate to me. You forfeited that right last weekend. Now go away and leave me alone.'

'You criticize *my* behaviour! How do I know what *you've* been up to while I was away? For all I know you could have been

198

sneaking down here night after night.'

'And if I have,' Tamily flared. 'Whose fault would that be? You should have come home and looked after me yourself. Don't you think I got bored, bored, bored down here on my own? Only Mother and Mercia for company. Don't you think I needed a little excitement, too? Don't you think I was ever lonely? But you wouldn't care about what I feel—you just want everything to suit yourself. You always did, Dick. Even as a little boy everything had to be your way. But this time, you've gone too far. I've had enough.'

Dick listened appalled. Somewhere at the back of his mind he accepted her accusations as fair. But that Tamily—his Tamily—should be talking to him like this...he just couldn't understand it. She couldn't really mean to leave him.

'Look, Tamily, I'll grant I may not have been a particularly good husband, but I do love you, I—'

'Love?' Tamily repeated the word in a voice full of derision. 'Do you call the petty little desire you have love? You don't know the meaning of the word, Dick. Loving means giving—not taking. If your kind of love is all you have to offer I'm not sure

I wouldn't prefer Adam's.'

'Okay!' Dick's head flung back indignantly. 'If that's what you want—you can have him!' And he turned on his heel and made for the door. In the doorway he hesitated, waiting for the sound of Tamily's voice. Surely she would stop him going? Tam never allowed a quarrel to linger on. She would always weaken at the last minute and come running to him. But this time she did not move.

As soon as she ceased to hear Dick's footsteps Tamily looked up at Adam.

'I'm so sorry,' she said. 'And I'm so ashamed—for Dick and for myself. It was unforgivable to inflict a scene like that upon you. And what I said...I ought not to have made up a lie like that. But I was so hurt...I wanted to hurt him. I'm sorry, Adam!'

Within a moment he was on his knees beside her, her small cold hands held tightly in his own.

'Since we're having some home truths you might as well know that it wasn't a lie, Tamily. I do love you—very, very much. I ought not to be saying this but maybe it will be some comfort to know that one man, however useless and helpless, thinks you the most wonderful woman he has ever met.'

Tamily bit her lip. This was apparently a day for shocks. Adam's words stunned her into silence. She hadn't once thought he might be falling in love with her....

'Oh, Adam, I'm so sorry!' she whispered. 'I ought to have thought—to have guessed....'

He stood up, smiling down at her. Then walked away from her, not daring to stay so close.

'No, I did everything in my power to hide it from you. I was afraid if you found out I would lose your friendship. As long as there was ignorance there was innocence. Now Dick's jealousy has taken it beyond that possibility. He couldn't believe we were simply friends—and maybe he is right. I don't think any man could spend much time in your company without falling in love with you.'

She did not know what to say. Affection and pity combined with an aching need for the love he offered her. After Dick's defection it was incredibly comforting to know that she was not dull and unattractive and unworthy of love. Was it possible that she could grow to love Adam? Aloud she said:

'I have loved Dick all my life. I don't know if I can stop loving him—even after what he has done.'

'My dear, I hope you can't. I couldn't marry you even if you were free and wanted me to take care of you. I'm not going to be able to take care even of myself. Besides, Tamily, you have Mercia and the new child to think of. I presume from what has just happened that Dick doesn't know you are going to have a baby?'

Tamily shook her head.

'How could I tell him? You know most of it, so you might as well know the rest. Dick spent last weekend in Cannes alone with that American girl who was here two weeks ago.'

'You mean he came home and told you about it?'

'No! Mr Holmer wrote him a letter and somehow the envelope was wrongly addressed to me. Apparently Dick had all but broken Carol's heart as well as spending a lot of her money. I...I'm ashamed of him...ashamed to talk about it.'

Adam drew a long sigh. In a way the news did not come as such a surprise to him. Young Allenton was, in many ways, very immature. At heart he was still at the undergraduate stage. And Carol Holmer had been very much out to attract. It wasn't so very surprising that Dick had been unable to withstand temptation. At the same time Adam could appreciate the shock to Tamily. Innocent as she was, this aspect of man's behaviour—the purely physical satisfaction of making love to an attractive woman—was no doubt beyond her comprehension. For her, love must always be of the mind as well as the body. She was an idealist, not a realist, and it must have come as a terrible shock.

He knew that *he* would not have done what Dick had done. But then his temperament was not Dick's. If he had been married to a girl like Tamily he would have settled down happily for the rest of his life, never wanting to touch another woman. But he could see that part of Dick's attraction for Tamily was his boyish, wayward charm. Take that away and turn him into a reliable, steady husband and he was no longer Dick.

This was not the moment to try to make her see the truth. It was too soon—and she was still too hurt. He said gently:

'As you don't want to go home, I'm going to take you up to the Manor. Your mother can look after you better there, can't she? Have a few days in bed—a complete rest, and all this will seem much less terrible. It might even be a good idea to have Dr Parker up to give you a check over. Will you do as I say, Tamily?'

She nodded.

'I'll do anything you want, Adam—just as long as I don't have to see Dick.'

He slipped his jacket over her shoulders for she was shivering and led her slowly up the drive to the big house.

10

'If you only knew how sorry I am!' Carol said softly. 'Dad, too, is overcome with remorse. He said to tell you that if there is anything at all he can do to put matters right he'll do it.'

Dick shrugged his shoulders helplessly. He sat in the armchair in the comfortable sitting-room of the Holmers' hotel suite. Carol, cool and remote, sat opposite him. It was Monday afternoon. Dick had finished early after a busy day and had been about to go home to the flat when Carol telephoned him.

'Will you come and have tea with me at our hotel?' she had asked, her voice serious and, as far as Dick could make out, very repentant. 'Dad told me what happened at the weekend. We both want to apologize.'

At first Dick had been about to refuse. There seemed little point in the Holmers' apologizing. The harm could not be undone. But Carol insisted that he owed her the chance to say how sorry she was—although, naturally, it had not been *her* mistake.

'I know that, Carol! I don't blame you.'

'Then at least show you don't hold it against me,' Carol had begged. 'I should hate us to part with this between us.'

Dick dreaded the idea of going back to his empty flat. He hadn't wanted to come to London at all, but his parents and Jess advised him that he was best out of the way until Tamily was calmer. He felt guilty and injured at the same time: guilty because he knew he had hurt Tamily desperately; injured because somehow she had let the whole family know that he had betrayed her.

She'd had no right to blurt it all out to Bond. He wasn't even a member of the family. But then Dick wasn't to know just how far Tamily's friendship with Bond had progressed. For all he knew they had been on as intimate terms as he and Carol! Not that he really believed this—it just wasn't like Tam to behave like that. No, in a way it was far worse; Tam was obviously *fond* of the man and when Tam became emotionally involved then it could be a good deal more far-reaching than his own casual affair with Carol....

Tamily had stayed all weekend at the manor house and refused to see him. Dick spent the remainder of Saturday and Sunday moping round his garden without even little Mercia for company, Jess having taken her up to the house so she could look after Tamily and the child under the same roof.

Sunday evening, he was packing to leave for London when his father paid him a surprise visit.

'See here, Dick, I have something to say to you. As you know, it isn't my policy to interfere in your private affairs but this time I feel it is my duty to do so. I understand from your mother that you suddenly reverted to your irresponsible young bachelor days. Well, it just isn't good enough, my boy. I'm not having Tamily put in this humiliating position just because you are a spoilt young puppy with no self-control and no appreciation of what's worth while in life. Tamily is too good for you—far too good, and always has been.

You were lucky to get such a wife. If she

walks out on you now I shouldn't blame her one little bit.'

Because he knew his father's remarks were justified Dick was sullen and aggressive. He said:

'I'm not a child any longer, Father. You can't dictate what I'm to do or not do!'

'No more I can, Dick. But I'm telling you this much—if Tamily gives you another chance—and to my way of thinking it is a very big "if"—if she does and you repeat your infidelities I'm cutting you off. Go ahead and call me Victorian if you wish. I know I can't stop you inheriting the title, but, believe me, my boy, I'll leave you without a penny. I shall make it all over to Tamily....'

Dick preferred not to remember the disgusted expression on his father's face. No one seemed to be in the least inclined to see *his* point of view. It hadn't been his fault Holmer had blundered and let the cat out of the bag. Why, the way his family were behaving, one would think he was in the habit of taking girls away for weekends, whereas in fact Carol had been the first—and he'd been sorry enough about it afterwards. No one bothered to enquire if he didn't feel badly about the affair and had little need of their recriminations. Since they preferred to look on him as the proverbial 'black sheep', he might as well be hung for one, he decided sulkily. He'd go and have tea with the Holmers, and even though he certainly did not intend to get involved with Carol again, it would at least be some slight balm to his wounded feelings to hear their apologies. God knows they were deserved! If he'd thought for one minute that sending the letter to Tam had been a deliberate mistake—and not just a ghastly blunder—he'd have killed Holmer with his bare hands!

Carol broke in on his thoughts. She said:

'Isn't there something I can do, Dick? Maybe if I wrote to your wife and said it was all my fault...'

Dick looked at her with surprise. This was a new Carol—someone he hadn't believed capable of considering anybody's desires but her own.

'That's decent of you, Carol,' he said with more warmth in his tone than he'd used since he'd arrived. 'But it would only make things worse. It takes two to commit adultery, you know!'

Carol took out the cigarette-holder Dick had given her and lit a cigarette. She regarded Dick through the smoke.

'I suppose it was a pretty ghastly shock for your wife,' she said thoughtfully. 'All the same, if she really loves you so much she might try to see your point of view as well as her own.'

Dick sighed.

'You say that because you don't know Tam. She isn't capable of understanding how a chap could be tempted. Love and sex are inseparable in her mind. She could no more enjoy sex without love than I could a whisky without any soda.'

Carol gave another shrug of her shoulders.

'I don't see how you ever came to marry a girl like that,' she said. 'Attraction of opposites?'

'Maybe!' Dick grinned. 'I know I'm a bad hat—unreliable and weak and a sucker for lovely women.'

His face grew more serious.

'The fact is, Carol, I do love Tammy. If I'd thought for one single instant that she'd find out about us I'd never, never have gone away with you. The whole plan seemed safe enough. It *would* have been all right if only your father—'

'It was that wretched temporary secretary of his!' Carol broke in quickly. 'I warned Dad against employing someone casual from an agency. There's no knowing if you can trust them. But Dad said he was piled up with correspondence and must have someone...'

Dick frowned.

'I still don't see how she could have been mistaken about that envelope. The contents of the letter must have made it obvious it was intended for a man, not a woman.'

'I know!' Carol agreed hastily. 'I took that point up with her when Dad called her to account for what she'd done. She just said it wasn't her business to question what was in a letter and that Dad had said "*Mrs* Allenton" and that was all she was concerned with. Of course, Dad asked could she prove he'd said "*Mrs*" from her shorthand notes, but she said she hadn't kept her notes after Dad had signed the letters—so, you see, we've no come-back.'

'There's no come-back anyway!' Dick said helplessly. 'Even if your father could prove her wrong it doesn't undo the harm.'

'What are you going to do about it, Dick?'

'What can I do? It's up to Tam now.'

'Do you think she'll ask for a divorce?'

Until that moment Dick had not considered the possibility seriously. Now, hearing the words from Carol's lips, he was suddenly terribly afraid. Suppose Tam didn't get over it! Suppose she did decide to divorce him! Last week he would not have thought this in the least probable, but now there was Adam Bond to contend with. Just what did the man mean to Tamily?

He was a decent enough chap if one was going to be fair—or, at any rate, he'd always seemed so in the past. And good-looking. He hadn't much money, but then Tam had never demanded a high standard of living. She was quite content with a simple life—the kind of life Bond could give her, quiet, country living. It wasn't even as if he and Tam had children to keep them tied together. Mercia was theirs, of course, but now he had forfeited his right to the child.

'It's a bloody awful mess!' he said violently. 'And the worst of it is, Carol, there isn't a thing I can do about it.'

'If I'd been married to you, Dick, I'd

never have let you off the leash for a long weekend. Frankly, I don't see how your wife can have been so naïve as to accept your story that Father was going along with us. Surely she must have had suspicions...'

Dick felt an implied criticism.

'It wouldn't occur to Tam to doubt my word. She trusted me.'

'Was that quite fair to you, Dick? In a way it's taking you for granted, isn't it? She was so sure of you in her mind that she didn't think you might be getting a bit bored with domesticity and need a change.'

This aspect had not occurred to Dick. He'd felt entirely to blame and the feeling was objectionable. It was some relief to think that maybe Tamily was, however slightly, also at fault. Carol was right. If Tam really loved him all that much why hadn't she kicked up a fuss when he'd told her he was going away? She had taken his love entirely for granted, otherwise she would have suspected he was up to something.

But an innate fairness made him re-member that Tam *had* been jealous of Carol; that he'd only convinced her the trip abroad was vital when he'd explained he dare not offend the Holmers because of the money he hoped to make out of them and how this might succeed in bringing nearer their hopes of starting up the farm.

'Hell, I feel guilty as hell!' he said aloud. 'I wouldn't blame Tam for walking out on me.'

Carol realized she was not going to succeed in making Tamily less desirable by trying to throw the blame on her. She swung round to another tack.

'I suppose once she is free she'll marry that bailiff of your father's?'

Dick's head jerked up.

'What makes you think that?'

'Oh, I don't know!' She purposefully kept her voice casual. 'The way the two of them behaved when I was down at your house, I suppose. He couldn't keep his eyes off her...and it was obvious she liked him—the way she stayed behind when we went up to coffee at the Manor; the way they were sitting in the dark when we got back. Remember?'

'But they'd been playing records and—'

'Naturally they weren't going to admit to anything else, were they? Frankly, Dick,

214

I think you're taking this whole business a lot too much to heart. It isn't Tamily who is being naïve, but you. You have this idea fixed in your mind that she's one hundred per cent the innocent, sweet, loving little wife. Couldn't you be just the littlest bit off the beam? Couldn't she be just a plain, ordinary woman with an ordinary woman's desires and temptations? Couldn't she, as well as you, have been finding domesticity just the smallest bit dull and wanting a change? Maybe it was very convenient having you away for the weekend, huh?'

'That's utterly ridiculous!' Dick said hotly. 'You just don't know Tam!'

But Carol was wise enough not to press the point. Dick might jump to Tamily's defence but the seeds of doubt were sown. He wouldn't be able to rid himself of the suspicion Carol had put into his mind.

That suspicion became magnified when next morning he received a letter from his wife.

Dear Dick,

As I am still not too well, I have decided to stay here at the Manor for a little while. Unless you particularly wish to spend the weekends by yourself at Lower Beeches I intend to shut the house up for a week or two until I feel strong enough to cope.

Perhaps you will let me know if it is not convenient for you to remain in London for the time being.

I realize, of course, that the Manor is your home, so if you wish to come here I will move back to Lower Beeches and then you can spend the weekends with your family.

It was signed simply with her name.

Dick flung the letter down on his desk with an angry gesture. She couldn't have made it any plainer that she didn't wish to see him! She might just as well have written: *Please keep out of my way!* As to her being ill—obviously that was just an excuse to put an end to their normal way of life.

His first instinct was to rush down and have it out with her. The tension was getting him down and even if he had to hear the worst he would rather *know* now than be kept on tenterhooks indefinitely waiting for her to make up her mind. But a second letter from Jess made him hesitate.

Dear Dick,

Tamily is not at all well and the doctor thinks it best that she stay here for a few days, where she can get all the rest she needs. She is in a highly emotional frame of mind and I think it would be better if you did not try to see her for a short while. Somehow I feel sure that once she is feeling physically fitter she will see what has happened between you in a different light.

Will you trust me to let you know when the time is right for you to suggest a fresh start together? To try to force the issue now would, I fear, be to court disaster.

Knowing you, I realize the waiting will not be easy but I would not have suggested it if I were not as sure as anyone could be that I am right in this.

Ever your affectionate,

Jess

Dick put the letter back in the envelope. He was not sure if Jess *was* right, but he appreciated her letter. As his mother-in-law, she had every right to send him an angry, accusing letter haranguing him for upsetting and hurting her daughter. But there had not been one criticism—only suggestions for patching up a marriage

217

which seemed hourly to be nearer and nearer to foundering.

He debated during the morning whether or not to accept Jess's advice. At last he came to the conclusion that it might be better than following his own instinct, which was to rush down and 'have it out'. His instincts were none too reliable, as he was too often discovering lately. They led him into difficulties he never anticipated. Jess knew Tamily pretty well. Maybe she was the better judge of what should be done next. At least her letter gave him hope for the future.

He lunched with the Holmers, who, he realized, were doing their best to make amends. Harry Holmer had tickets for a theatre for the three of them for Wednesday night and would not listen to Dick's half-hearted excuses for refusing to go. There was also tickets for them all for Wimbledon on Saturday. Dick was very much a tennis enthusiast and was sorely tempted. After all, if he had to spend the weekend in London he might as well be doing something interesting as moping in his flat, brooding over what had happened.

At least he felt a little less lonely and

depressed while he was at the theatre on Wednesday. The Holmers insisted they take him on to supper at Prunier's afterwards and he felt safe enough with Carol's father as chaperone. Even if they were seen together no one could accuse him of continuing his affair with Carol. That he had not the slightest intention, or desire, to do.

On Saturday he was only mildly disconcerted to hear from Carol that her father wasn't too well and wouldn't be going to watch the tennis. As far as Dick could see, Carol was no longer trying to attract him...her manner was friendly but distant. He felt in no danger and after only a second's hesitation he agreed to accompany her to Wimbledon without her father's chaperonage.

It seemed a perfectly innocent request when on the way back to central London, in the chauffeur-driven car the Holmers had hired, Carol suggested they stop off at Dick's flat for a drink.

'It's so terribly hot, Dick, and I hate pubs. I want something long and cool—with lots of ice in it.'

Again Dick's hesitation was only momentary. He had nothing to do for the rest of the evening. He could have asked Carol out to dinner, but he meant to avoid any possibility of a tête-à-tête with her. From now on their friendship could only continue if it was strictly platonic. But a drink...it hardly seemed civil to refuse.

'I promise not to stay more than a moment,' Carol said. 'Even if I wanted to linger on I couldn't, as I must get back to the hotel and see how Dad is.'

Dick nodded.

'A quick one, then!' he agreed, and led the way upstairs.

★ ★ ★ ★

'It's just no good, Mother—I love him. I can't pretend it's all over between us. I don't want to pretend. I just want him back!'

Jess sighed. There seemed no point in trying to make her daughter see the wisdom of teaching Dick a lesson. Tamily always had been and probably always would be weak as water where Dick was concerned. She loved him...she would forgive him anything.

'A day or two, at any rate!' she suggested.

Tamily was sitting up in bed. The colour was back in her cheeks and she looked very well but for darkish circles beneath her eyes. Dr Palmer had confirmed her pregnancy, given her pills to ease the sickness and told her she could get up when she felt like it.

The fact was, Tamily felt perfectly well now. The first terrible shock of learning that Dick had been unfaithful to her had worn off and she was recovering her sense of proportion as well as her normal good health. Of course, it would be some time before she could *forgive* Dick; maybe years before she would forget. But the plain truth was that she loved him in spite of his faults and she had not the slightest intention of divorcing him.

'I'm certainly not going to hand him over to Miss Carol Holmer on a plate!' she told her mother firmly. 'Perhaps that's just what that girl wanted. Well, she's going to be disappointed. If our marriage busts up it'll be because Dick walks out on me—not because I throw him over.'

'Don't be in too much of a hurry to forgive him, darling. He needs to learn his lesson—and he won't if he gets away with this too easily!'

'A few more days, then,' Tamily agreed. 'But I'm not wasting next weekend with him as well as the last. The one before that we had the Holmers down—it's nearly a whole month since Dick and I had a whole weekend quietly together.'

So for two more days she rested and sat in the sunshine and recovered her health. In the afternoons she wandered down to have tea with Adam. By tacit, silent agreement, the declaration of love he had made was not mentioned again between them. It was as if he had never told her that he loved her—except that she felt the warmth of his affection and friendship in the gentle, tender way in which he looked after her.

'Goodness, Adam—you've no need to fetch and carry for me. Having a baby isn't an illness, you know.'

Adam grinned.

'I ought to know well enough from nature—but somehow you seem so young and—well, vulnerable....'

It was the nearest he came to mentioning the way he felt about her. Both realized that it was only by ignoring what had been said that they could continue as friends. Tamily desperately wanted to be able to go on as before. Adam was one of the few friends she had, and apart from her need of him, she knew that he needed her, too; would perhaps need her even more when blindness finally descended on him.

On Friday she didn't stay long.

'I'm going up to London tomorrow, Adam,' she said gently. 'I'm going up to the flat to surprise Dick.'

She saw the apprehension on his face, and smiled.

'You don't have to look so worried. Dick isn't in the habit of shouting at me the way he did the other day. I have to go, Adam. You see, Dick isn't like you—you have to know him as well as I do to understand him. He doesn't mean to be selfish or hurtful. It's just that he's a bit weak and...well, I can see that that American girl was rather tempting. I know he didn't love her...and that's all that really counts in the long run. He's desperately sorry now. I didn't tell you, did I, that he has phoned Mother every night to ask if I'm all right and if she thought I'd consent to see him. That's why I thought up this idea of surprising him in London. I want to meet him halfway—not make him feel I'm having

him back on sufferance. Dick would hate
that...and hate me for making him feel in
the wrong.'

Adam Bond said thoughtfully:

'You must love him very much. Lucky
Dick!'

Tamily nodded.

'I have always loved him and I think
I always will. No matter what he does
he'll always be Dick, the boy I fell in
love with and married. I don't think I
could stop loving him even if I wanted
to.'

With some strange premonition of disaster Adam said:

'Suppose he isn't at the flat?'

'But of course he'll be there. He might
go out for a meal or something, but he
won't be going away. He'd have told
Mother if he'd meant to go to any of our
friends. I have a key to the flat, Adam.
If he isn't there I'll just let myself in and
wait for him.'

'Let me drive you to the station, then,'
Adam suggested, hiding his unaccountable
misgivings. 'What train will you catch?'

'The 2.30. It's fast!' Tamily said,
standing up and preparing to go. 'Thanks
for offering to drive me, Adam—I'll be

glad of the lift...and...thank you...for everything.'

The train reached London at 3.35. By the time she had taken a taxi to the flat it was nearly four. Her first disappointment at finding Dick out gave way to relief. Now she would have time to tidy her hair, freshen up her make-up and have a cup of tea to help her to calm down.

She wasn't exactly nervous, but there was an under-lying tension and excitement that she had not felt for a long while. She tried, as she sat drinking tea, watching the hands of the clock, to visualize Dick's face when he came in and found her there; tried to imagine their first words to each other. But each opening led them into each other's arms and it was this anticipated moment of reunion that was causing her heart-beat to quicken.

A little after five she heard the lift stopping at their floor. She was certain it was Dick and curbed a desire to run out to meet him. She remained seated in the chair, her hands trembling. Then there came the sound of a key in the lock and she knew it must be Dick.

No longer able to control herself, she

jumped to her feet and took a few steps forward. At that moment the door opened and Dick, his arm linked through Carol's, walked in.

11

For one long, interminable moment they stared at each other. Then Dick's face lit up and he started towards Tamily with an eager smile, forgetting Carol at his side. But as he stepped forward Tamily backed away. Afterwards she was to wonder how she was able to speak so coolly and firmly as she said:

'I came here to tell you I'm going to divorce you, Dick. My mind is made up finally and irrevocably.'

She bent down and picked up her bag and gloves.

Dick said:

'But, Tam...you can't...you mustn't... don't you know I love you, Tam?...'

She walked straight past him, ignoring him and nodded to Carol.

'He's all yours!' she said softly. 'And I hope he makes you a better husband than he's made me. I shall, of course, be naming you as co-respondent. I may possibly sue you for enticement...you can afford the

227

damages, can't you? Well, goodbye, both of you...and good luck!'

Dick came forward, but before he could touch her Tamily had disappeared through the open door, closing it firmly behind her.

'I won't let her go like that,' he almost shouted, but Carol stood between him and the door. She said coolly:

'Have a bit of pride, Dick! She didn't mean it, you know. She is just trying to hurt you.'

Dick hesitated, wondering if Carol was right.

'No, she did mean it!' he said at last. He pushed her out of the way and ran out into the hall. But he was too late. Tamily had already started on her way down in the lift. He thought of trying to race the lift by running downstairs, but he knew he would never make it in time. Slowly, he walked back to the flat.

Carol was pouring out drinks.

'Vindictive, isn't she?' she said calmly. 'Coming all this way just for the fun of kicking you out. How about your nice, sweet Tamily now!'

Dick looked at her with helpless anger.

'You don't know what you're talking

about. You don't realize what this means to me. Besides'...comprehension came to him suddenly....'Tam wouldn't have come all this way to tell me something she could have written in a letter. There's something behind her visit, something I don't understand. But I'm damn' well going to find out.'

He ignored the drink Carol held out and pushed past her into his bedroom, where he began to throw some clothes into a suitcase. Carol walked to the doorway and watched him, for the first time a look of consternation in her eyes.

'What are you doing? You're not going after her.'

'Yes, I am! I'm beginning to understand now. Tam came back because she wanted to make it up...and then she saw *you!* My God, Carol, this is *your* fault...if you hadn't been with me...'

'Dick, please. Listen to me. She doesn't really love you. This is just an excuse to be rid of you. She's in love with Bond...Dick, listen to me.'

But he was paying no attention to her words. When she tried again to stop him from leaving he looked at her coldly, saying:

'I'll take a taxi to the station, Carol. Can I drop you on the way?'

Carol's face became taut and ugly with fury. Her eyes a cold hard green, she flashed at him:

'If you go after her I'll never speak to you again, Dick. I mean it. You don't want her—you don't need a woman like that. Dick—listen to me. I'll fight the case if she divorces you....I'll ruin her reputation. Dick, you've got to listen. I can give you far more than she can...anything in the world you want. *Dick...*'

He saw her for the first time in her true colours and he felt sickened—not so much with disgust for her, but for himself. That he could have betrayed Tam for this... He couldn't even find a suitable name for her.

'Goodbye, Carol!' he said with as much politeness as he could muster. 'I don't suppose we shall meet again.'

She stood watching him, her face a mask of helpless fury as he walked out of her life. She knew she had lost the game and would never see him again.

Dick was too late to catch Tamily's train and had to wait half an hour before the next one. Consequently, he did not arrive at Allenton Halt until after the accident. The ticket-collector, who had known Dick since he was a boy, broke the news to him.

'It's your wife, sir, she's had an accident. She fell getting out of the carriage. They've took her to the Cottage Hospital in the ambulance.... I telephoned to the big house and told them. They'll be over at the hospital by now, I reckon.'

White-faced, Dick ordered the station taxi to drive him straight to the hospital, which was fifteen miles away at Wilstown. Every mile seemed to take an hour and even the promise of a pound tip could not make the taxi-driver put up more than 30 m.p.h. on the speedometer.

The ticket-collector had been unable to give Dick any information about Tamily's condition. As far as the old man knew, there'd been no broken bones. All he would say was that her injuries must have been internal, for she'd been in great distress; that was why he'd phoned for the ambulance.

Now that he was trapped in the taxi Dick began to wish he'd taken time to telephone home for news. But it was not worth stopping now. He chain-smoked, constantly urging the driver to go faster, regardless of the dangers of speeding in the narrow winding lanes through which they passed.

He was out of the car even before it stopped and raced up the hospital steps. Silently he was praying: 'Don't let Tamily be seriously ill. Oh, God, don't let her be dead!'

The girl at the reception desk looked at his anxious face and said soothingly:

'If you'll just wait a few minutes, Mr Allenton, I'll find out about your wife.'

Then he felt a hand on his arm and Jess's voice was saying:

'So you heard the news, Dick. I didn't expect to see you here. Tamily said—'

'She has it all wrong, Jess. I'll explain in a minute. But first tell me how she is? What happened? For pity's sake, Jess, put me in the picture.'

Jess took him into the waiting-room which fortunately was empty. She forced him into a chair.

'It wasn't your fault, Dick, so get that off your mind to begin with. It was an accident. She slipped as she got out of the carriage and fell on to the platform. There's nothing broken and she's going to be all right. The only question is whether or not she'll lose the baby.'

'Lose...the...baby?' Dick echoed stupidly. Jess nodded.

'I'm not supposed to have told you about the baby, but it seems to me, Dick, that it is high time you knew. After all, it is your child, too.'

Dick was too stunned to speak for a few moments. Then, as Jess's words sank in, he gripped her arm, saying:

'Will she lose the child? What does the doctor say? Can I see her?'

Jess's face looked tired and worried.

'I'm afraid Tamily doesn't want to see you, Dick. I gather things between you are worse than ever. Perhaps you'd better try to explain what happened in London. The only thing I know is that she went up to the flat today to tell you she was willing to start anew; then you walked in with the Holmer girl.'

Dick looked at his mother-in-law, his face earnest and anxious.

'That's perfectly true—Carol was with me. We'd been to Wimbledon—her father gave us tickets. I was bored and miserable and worried to death about Tam and I couldn't see any harm in going to a tennis

233

tournament. Honestly, Jess, I give you my solemn word of honour there was nothing more in it than that. I admit to being unfaithful to Tammy before; I admit to being weak and all the rest of the sordid business of a brief affair. But I never intended to let it begin again. I haven't even kissed Carol since we stepped off the plane at London Airport.'

'Then what was Miss Holmer doing in your flat this evening?'

'She stopped on her way home for a quick drink. It was a terribly hot day—you know that, Jess. We were both dying for something cool and Carol hates pubs. One quick drink—that was all either of us intended—and then as we walked in I saw Tam there. Jess, you have to believe me because it's the plain truth. I may be a cheat but I'm not a liar. You know that.'

Looking into his eyes, Jess believed him. What he had said was the truth. Even as a mischievous small boy Dick had never told lies. He always owned up to his pranks and took the consequences without complaint.

'I'll try to make Tamily believe you,' she said gently. 'But I can't promise I'll succeed. All I do know is that she loves you and she has had two nasty shocks.

234

Now this accident...I just don't know how she'll react.'

Dick breathed a sigh of relief.

'Thanks, Jess!' he said. 'You've every right to refuse to help me—after the way I've hurt Tam. But you've got to believe that I never meant to hurt her. I never meant her to *know*. Why in God's name didn't she tell me about the baby? If I'd known I'd never, never have taken Carol to France.'

Jess looked at him with a certain amount of sympathy.

'You'd gone before she *could* tell you,' she said quietly. 'Afterwards.... Well, she didn't feel like telling you.'

Dick put his head in his hands.

'You don't know what kind of a skunk I feel!' he said miserably. 'I hope to God she doesn't lose the baby.'

Jess looked at the bowed head with dawning hope. For the first time in his life Dick was thinking of Tamily first. Maybe there was hope for the marriage, after all. Maybe she could persuade Tammy to believe Dick had had no intention of reopening the affair with Carol.

'Better come home, Dick!' she said gently. 'Tamily's sleeping now. In any case you wouldn't be allowed to see her. She's got to have absolute quiet.'

Jess tried to explain that Tamily needed all her strength to win the fight to keep the baby. This wasn't the time for recriminations or emotional scenes.

'At least she still wants the baby, then!' Dick said wretchedly. 'Despite the fact that it is mine!'

He slept little that night and his nerves were very much on edge. He had never felt more unhappy; more powerless to help himself. Perhaps for the first time in his life, he felt certain he had lost Tamily's love and regard. It was all the more bitter to take now that he knew she had been prepared for a reconciliation when she had come up to his flat. This time, he was innocent of wrong-doing and it was consequently the harder to accept that their marriage had come to an end through no continued fault of his.

His father and mother watched him covertly, but he made no effort to talk to them. The office had allowed him compassionate leave which, under the circumstances, was unfortunate. He might have been able to better pass the time if he had had work to do. Sensing this, his father said:

'Bond is short-handed this week, Dick. Two of the men are on holiday. How about seeing Bond, asking if there's anything you can do to help?'

Dick's first instinct was to refuse. He was damned if he was going to offer his services to his wife's lover! But a masochistic desire to know the worst finally drove him to follow his father's suggestion. Perhaps he would learn from Bond if Tamily really wanted a divorce and intended to marry *him*.

Adam, however, was not at the Lodge. The young chap who drove the tractor was in the field behind the drive. He informed Dick that Bond was in the bull-pen.

Dick wandered across the fields to the farm buildings. Since Bond's arrival here as bailiff these had been completely modernized and the place was now a model farm—all painted a uniform white and green, equipped with modern machinery and labour-saving aids which had helped the estate to make a profit instead of a loss. Now one of the best Jersey herds in the country was housed here and Bond had been doing very well these last years with the breeding. He had a prize bull which he still preferred to use rather than the artificial insemination methods chosen by most farmers. The bull was Adam's prize exhibit when his father brought friends up here to see the herd.

Adam was in the pen, approaching the great beast, as Dick walked up to the exercise yard where he was kept. Dick watched, his mind diverted for a moment from his own worries by the angry tossing of the bull's head and the wicked glint in his eye. Nasty, dangerous-looking specimen, he thought. But obviously the animal had a healthy respect for the man coming towards him.

Suddenly, as Dick watched, Adam hesitated, his step faltered and he stood still, his hand going up first to his head and then down to his eyes. He swayed, looked as if he might fall and then stumbled forward a few steps.

'Watch out, Bond!' Dick cried as he saw the bull's head go up and his ears flatten backwards on his head.

Adam seemed not to hear him. Again Dick called, and now the bull had lowered his head, his eyes still fixed on Adam's swaying figure.

'Bond!' Dick shouted, and vaulted over the high concrete wall just as the beast charged.

For a moment there was terrible confusion as the two men and the vicious animal came together. There was a muffled gasp of pain from Adam as the bull's horn tore into the side of his leg just as Dick pulled him sideways. The bull turned and prepared to rush a second time. Seeing the danger, Dick heaved the older man on to his feet and, half pushing, half pulling, shoved him up and over the wall. As he himself sprang upwards he heard the snorting of the animal behind him and felt its hot breath on his legs.

Then he hit the ground with a thud and for a second or two he knew nothing.

'Are you all right, sir?'

It was the cowman, helping Dick to his feet. Dick felt his bruised body and nodded.

'Where's Bond?' he asked stupidly. Then he saw him, lying on the ground, the blood seeping slowly from the nasty wound in his leg.

Together Dick and the cowman did a rough first-aid job, staunching the gaping wound with one rolled handkerchief and tying it in place with another. Then they carried him into the nearby hay barn and laid him down. The man's face was ashen; his eyes were closed.

'Quick, man—ring Dr Parker first, then the Manor. He'll have to go to hospital. I'll stay here with him.'

The cowman ran off towards the dairy where the telephone had recently been connected. Dick sat beside Adam and tried to remember just what had happened. It didn't make sense. Why had Bond hesitated—almost as if he were afraid? Was he ill? He must have known that was no way to approach the bull.

Suddenly Adam opened his eyes. As consciousness returned he grimaced with pain. He turned his head slowly and saw Dick looking at him. He attempted a smile.

'Thanks!' he said. 'You saved my life!'

'How are you feeling now?' Dick asked, but already the man had drifted back into a state of oblivion.

It seemed an interminable wait before Dr Parker arrived. Adam was intermittently conscious and was given a shot of morphia before the leg was dressed.

'It'll have to be stitched!' Dr Parker

said. 'Needs some pretty expert attention. Reckon we'd better get him into the General at Wilstown. The Cottage Hospital won't have facilities to deal with this.'

'I'll come along with you,' Dick offered, but the doctor shook his head.

'You look as if you could do with a rest and a stiff drink,' he said. 'Shock's a funny thing—can have some nasty after-effects—so take it easy.'

Dick discovered the doctor was right. For an hour he couldn't stop shivering. It was only when Jess tucked him into bed with a hot-water bottle that he began to feel warm again; only then that he learned from Jess what Tamily had known for some time—that Adam Bond was on the verge of going blind.

12

When Dick answered the doorbell he was alone at Lower Beeches. Jess was at the hospital and had promised to phone him the instant there was any news. As he rushed to open the front door it was at the back of his mind that Jess might have terrible news for him and had come to break it in person rather than by phone.

His heart was thudding violently in his chest as he flung open the door. His mouth fell open when he saw the woman standing there.

'You!' he said to Carol. 'What are *you* doing here?'

She gave him a barely perceptible smile.

'That's not very polite, Dick. Aren't you going to ask me in?'

For a moment or two Dick could not reconcile himself to accepting that this was Carol and not Jess. He was relieved and angry at the same time. With an effort he pulled himself together and said:

'No, I'm not asking you in, Carol. I

thought I made it quite clear yesterday that I never wanted to see you again.'

Carol shrugged her shoulders. As usual, she was looking immaculate—cool and fresh in a smart linen two-piece.

'I only came to apologize to you and your wife. I thought it might help if I could explain to Tamily that we really were only having a drink together and—'

'Tamily's not here—she's in hospital!' Dick broke in roughly. 'It's a bit late for apologies, Carol.'

Carol looked genuinely surprised.

'But I don't understand. Hospital? But why?'

Dick sighed.

'I suppose you might as well come in,' he said. 'We can't stand here talking.'

He led the way into the drawing-room and automatically went to the sideboard to pour drinks. Carol watched him narrowly. She was no longer at all certain of her ground. Was it possible that Tamily had tried to commit suicide? Was there any chance now of her, Carol, getting hold of Dick for herself? She had about given up hope after the interlude in the flat...but now her hopes were beginning to rise again.

'Please tell me, Dick. I'm so worried about your wife. What happened?'

Dick handed her a glass and sat down opposite her and took a long drink.

'It was an accident!' he said, and told her briefly how Tamily had fallen when getting out of the train on her way back from Town.

'Is she badly hurt, then?'

'No, hardly at all. But she is pregnant and I never knew. Now the doctors aren't sure if they can save the child. I'm waiting for news from the hospital.'

Carol could not hide the sudden frown of disappointment. A baby—that was the last thing she had thought of...and it lowered her chances even further. Feeling her way, she said:

'How awful, Dick. But, you know, you mustn't blame yourself. After all, you didn't know she was pregnant, did you? And, besides, we weren't doing anything wrong—it was just all very unfortunate.'

'No, it was more than that!' Dick replied quietly, staring shamefacedly at his drink. 'I should have been here with Tam, looking after her. If it hadn't been for our so-called holiday in France, Tam would have told me about the baby. If she loses the child it will be my fault and I know it. Tamily will never forgive me. Oh, I wish to God Jess would phone.'

'Calm down!' Carol said laconically. 'I'm sure Tamily will be all right. As to the child—she can always have another one, can't she. I should imagine a baby at this time would only complicate things anyway. I mean, suppose she does want to leave you and marry Bond? It would be very awkward if she was having your baby, wouldn't it?'

Dick looked even more miserable. The mention of Bond's name in connection with Tamily would have made him furiously jealous in the ordinary way. But now, with poor Tam lying ill in hospital, he could only remember that Bond had been a friend when he, Tam's husband, had failed her. Bond deserved Tamily far more than he did. That was the hardest truth to bear. If he, Dick, really loved Tam he would probably get out of her life now—go off to America with Carol if needs be, but leave Tam free to marry a man worthy of her.

He tried to find comfort from Jess's assurance that Tamily still loved him, despite all his faults and the way he had continually hurt her. But he wouldn't blame her one little bit for preferring Bond. If she lost the baby she would hate him, Dick; blame him as well she might for the loss of her baby.

He put down his drink and put his head in his hands. If only Jess would phone.

'Dick!'

He looked up, remembering suddenly that Carol was there. He had all but forgotten her. With sudden anger, he said:

'You'd better go, Carol. There's nothing you can do.'

'I can't leave you alone here like this!' Carol said at once. 'Let me pour you another drink, Dick. You look awful—worn out.'

'I don't want another drink,' Dick said sighing. 'I just want to know that Tam and the baby are all right. Why doesn't Jess phone? It's been twenty-four hours—surely the doctors must know one way or the other by now.'

Carol's mouth tightened as she felt her hopes slipping even more surely away. This was the picture of a man deeply in love with his wife. He couldn't care less about *her*. Maybe she was mad to go on pursuing what looked like a hopeless case. Even if

Tamily turned against him Dick would probably blame her, Carol, for her part in breaking up the marriage. And there wasn't much happiness to be had in living with a man who positively disliked you.

She remembered her father's words to her that morning—strangely harsh words coming from him.

'You know, my dear, you'd far better come to Europe with me. Dick isn't for you. Deep down, you've known that all along. I don't even know if I am willing to help you any more to get what you want. I think we would be doing a very wrong thing in breaking up a marriage, however weak a partner Dick may be. To tell you the truth, I liked young Tamily. I did think at one time that money might compensate her for the loss of her husband, but it seems to me that she is putting up quite a fight for him. Don't go on with it, my dear. Come away with me and we'll find another young man you'll want even more than Dick Allenton.'

It was the first time in her life that Carol had known her father set himself against her wishes. Until now he had always been willing to give her whatever she wanted. Now, although the moral questions he raised were of no consequence, she was frightened by his acceptance of failure. If her father thought it improbable she would succeed then it was indeed very improbable.

But a ruthless kind of determination prompted her to make one more effort...to go to the house and find out for herself if Dick's wife had forgiven him, or if she had had too much and had walked out on him. If this latter were true then she would be nicely placed to pick up the pieces....

She had not known then about the accident, or the fact that Tamily was pregnant. Now she was left with only one last hope—not that Dick would leave his wife—but that his wife would leave him.

She decided to put on a 'good friends' act. She went across to Dick and laid her arm along his shoulders.

'Don't worry so, Dick,' she said in her softest voice. 'I'm sure she'll be all right. You know what the saying is—no news is good news.'

Oblivious to Carol's proximity, Dick sighed and said:

'I wish I could make myself believe that. All the time I have this horrible feeling that Tam's going to lose that baby and she'll blame me. What's more, I know she has every right to do so. I don't know how she has put up with me for so long anyway. I've been a rotten husband.'

Carol hid the feeling of exasperation she now felt. This remorseful self-pitying young man was far from being the gay, amusing, ardent companion she had wanted to marry.

'Snap out of it, honey!' she said with more bite than she had intended. 'There's no point whatever in torturing yourself over suppositions. If your wife has had enough of you—then that'll be that. Even that isn't the end of the world. There are thousands of marriages breaking up right now, I dare say, and most of the people concerned will remarry and make perfectly happy lives for themselves.'

Dick looked up at Carol with a puzzled frown.

'You don't seem to understand, Carol. I love Tamily...*I don't want to lose her.* I know I don't deserve her but I love her and want to stay married to her. It may not be the end of the world if she walks out on me but it will certainly be the end of happiness for me.'

Carol bit her lip, turning away from

Dick to hide her annoyance. She was getting nowhere and Dick in this mood was far from entertaining.

'Why don't we go out and have a drink? I suppose there are some hotels round here where we can be a little more gay? It would do you good, honey.'

Dick shook his head immediately.

'I can't leave here—Jess might phone while I'm out. Help yourself to another drink if you want one, Carol. And, incidentally, how did you get here? By car?'

'Sure! I borrowed Pop's hired Daimler.'

'Then I'd better call the driver in. It's terribly hot outside. He'll probably be longing for a beer.'

Carol tossed her head.

'Let him wait. That's what he's being paid for.'

Dick gave her a long, searching stare.

'You are a selfish little bitch, aren't you, Carol? No thought for anyone but yourself.'

His criticism was the last straw. Her eyes were cold and flashing with anger as she said:

'That's a fine remark coming from you. Here I am after a long hot drive all the way from London just because I was worried about *you* and you accuse me of thinking of no one but myself. Seems to me, Dick, that you're the selfish one.'

Dick shrugged.

'Okay—so I'm selfish, too. We both are. And frankly, Carol, I don't see the point of you making the trip in the first place. I told you in the flat that I didn't want to see you again. I meant it.'

Her eyes narrowed and her mouth took on a cruel twist of frustration.

'If I go now I'll never see you again, Dick. It'll be the final end of our...our friendship.'

Dick looked back at her without flinching.

'We were never friends, Carol—only for a brief while lovers. I don't think I ever liked you very much and I don't suppose you liked me. I'm sorry if I've spoiled your trip to England—I didn't mean to mess things up for you. But if you're fair you'll admit that it was you who had made the running in the first place. I warned you the first day that I was married and had no intention of leaving my wife.'

'So you did!' Carol's voice was heavy with sarcasm. 'The honest little English aristocrat, aren't you, Dick? Well, I think you're rotten and Pop was right, after all—I'm stupid to waste my time on you. You aren't worth it.'

She stubbed out her cigarette and with a last narrowed look at the man she had tried so hard to ensnare she turned and walked out of the room. Dick made a single step towards her—good manners which were so much an innate part of him prompting him at least to show her out of his house. But then he paused. Better let her go—the sooner she was away from his sight and out of his life, the better he would be satisfied.

As he listened to the sound of the car purring into the distance, he sat down heavily in a chair, feeling mentally and emotionally as well as physically exhausted. Looking back over these last few months, he could no longer understand how he had ever been crazy enough to let his acquaintance with Carol Holmer develop as it had. He must have been blind not to see her for what she was. And even if she had been in character as attractive as she was in appearance, he was still crazy to have taken such risks with his marriage.

'Oh, Tam!' he all but groaned her name

aloud. 'I hope to God you're all right. Jess, why don't you phone?'

He remembered Bond, too, was lying in hospital. Poor devil! It must be pretty ghastly to know you would soon be totally blind, utterly dependent upon other human beings to get around at all.

It had been a nasty shock hearing that piece of news from Jess. He was probably the last one to hear about it! That showed, if nothing else did, how he had separated himself from his home and responsibilities.

Gloomily, Dick considered the future. He was still jealous of Tamily's friendship with Bond but somehow he could not bring himself to believe that she really loved the man. He could, however, well understand that her pity might have been evoked. It was just like Tam to feel personally involved in someone else's misfortune and to feel a burning need to do something about it. She might now want to marry Bond simply to look after him....

At this point Dick felt he had really touched rock bottom. He was no longer certain that he had any right to stand in Tam's way if this was indeed what she wanted. His instinct was to fight to keep her but he realized, too, that Bond needed her in a way he never had or probably ever would. Women liked to be needed—he knew that. And Tam, though he often forgot the fact, was all woman.

Dick sighed, allowing his mind to roam back into the past. Maybe the trouble with his relationship with Tam was due to the fact that they had shared their childhood. She'd been so much his companion then—not male nor female but just his friend. She knew his faults and helped him out of scrapes and was always there when he needed her. The idea of *her* needing *him* had never entered his mind.

'Selfish!' Carol had called him. And how right that was. Even after their marriage he hadn't really changed in his treatment of Tam. She always seemed so happy to fall in with his plans and schemes and had never given voice to her own. Blindly, he had assumed that was enough for her—to be his wife, there when he needed her. What had he put into the partnership? Practically nothing! No wonder she had had enough, for he had shown her clearly enough that he didn't in the least value her devotion. Nor was it any good trying to blame Carol for what had happened.

He had been weak, taking exactly what he wanted without the tiniest desire to give something up because it was unfair or disloyal to his wife; belittling to his marriage.

At last Dick could no longer stand his own thoughts. He was in the process of growing up and he found it too painful to endure the picture he was forced to paint of himself. He knew that if he were in Tamily's shoes he would not forgive.

He went into the hall and lifted the phone.

13

Jess looked down at the man with a deep, warm pity.

'How are you feeling, Adam?'

His head was heavily bandaged and he could see nothing. Beneath the bedclothes his leg was in plaster.

'A bit bruised!' he said honestly. 'But thanks to Allenton I reckon I got off fairly lightly. A broken bone, a few stitches and some bruises. I'm well aware I could have been gored to death.'

Jess sat down beside him and placed her hand over his.

'It was madness to go into that bull-pen, Adam, knowing your sight was failing.'

He nodded.

'I know. I just didn't realize it would happen so quickly. I'm very conscious of the fact that I unwittingly endangered Dick's life as well as my own. But I didn't want to give up work until I was forced to do so. I suppose that was selfish. If I'd told Lord Allenton he'd have retired me.

I wanted everything to go on as usual for a long as possible.'

'I think that's very human, Adam, and you mustn't blame yourself for what might have happened. Dick's perfectly all right—not a mark on him.'

'Yes, the doctor told me. It was nice of you to come, Jess. I...I badly wanted news of Tamily.'

Jess was glad Adam could not see the expression of pity even more marked on her face. As gently as possible, she told him:

'She's much better, Adam—and she hasn't lost the baby. In fact, the doctor said this morning that she was quite out of the wood. I'm here because she asked me to come—she would have liked to come herself, but of course she won't be allowed up for at least a week. She thought that was too long to leave you without news.'

'News?' Adam's voice was very low; Jess had to strain to hear the words.

'Yes, Adam, personal news. She said that she had confided in you about her problems with Dick; she also told me that you'd said you were in love with her. That gave you the right to know how she felt.'

Adam clenched his hands, his only

outward expression of his feelings that Jess might see. 'Dear Tamily,' he thought. 'She knows I've been lying here worrying and wondering about her.'

'Are they going to be all right?' he asked slowly. 'Dick and Tamily, I mean? I very much hope so.'

Jess let out her breath. She was immensely relieved to hear Adam say those words. Ever since Tamily had told her that Adam was in love with her she had been so afraid that one of the three of them was going to be badly hurt. Now it seemed that Adam was in no way counting on Tamily leaving Dick. Not that Jess disliked Adam—she was extremely fond of him and realized his intrinsic worth as a man. She respected him in a way it was impossible to respect Dick after his recent behaviour. But Jess knew life—knew that a woman's love did not necessarily repose where it was safest. Tamily still loved Dick and marriage to Adam would have been no more than a very second best. No matter what motives of pity and affection prompted such a union, Tamily would go on loving Dick and Adam would know it.

'Yes, Adam, it's going to be all right—given a little time. Dick has really

258

suffered these last few days. Tamily has agreed to see him this afternoon—until now she has refused to do so—I think because deep down she knows she will not be able to refuse forgiveness to his face. She knows her weakness! She is quite calm now—not a bit hysterical or over-wrought. It is as if she has resigned herself to accept Dick with all his short-comings. I think the baby will help—is helping already. She's very thrilled about it and it will divert some of her emotions away from Dick which will be better for them both. Her only real worry now is you.'

'Me? I'm all right, Jess. Please tell her so.'

'Yes, I know that you'll soon be recovered from your accident. But your approaching blindness, Adam. We are *all* deeply concerned about it.'

Adam turned his bandaged face towards Jess and said quietly:

'I will tell you this, Jess, on the condition that you do not mention it to Tamily until I am quite sure. Have I your promise?'

'Of course! Whatever you say will be in confidence.'

'Then I will tell you that I had a visit from the hospital consulting eye specialist this morning. He has taken X-rays of my head because it seems that there is some new technique just developed in America that might be the answer to my trouble. He has an American colleague visiting him who has given him full details. I should know almost at once if there really is a chance my sight can be saved.'

Jess's face was warm with pleasure.

'Why, that's marvellous news, Adam, *wonderful* news!'

'Yes! But you can see why I don't want to tell Tamily yet. She'd be so disappointed for me if it came to nothing. I hardly dare to hope myself, but I suppose deep down inside I am hoping. It looks as if this new operation has two or three times been performed in America successfully. In a way I will be a guinea-pig—it is still very experimental. But what have I got to lose? I'm going blind, anyway, so if the op. should fail I'm no worse off. Pray for me, Jess.'

'I will, I will. You'll let me know at once, Adam? If it is good news this will make so much difference to Tamily. She's very, very fond of you, you know.'

'Yes, I do know. I know, too, that what she feels for me is not love. She would not have given me a second thought if her marriage had been happy and fulfilling. I ought never to have told her that I loved her but it slipped out in an unguarded moment. But I'm not really sorry. Loving Tamily is nothing to be ashamed of. She's a wonderful person. Allenton is lucky.'

Jess stood up.

'Yes, and I think that at long last he is beginning to realize it. I shall have to go now, Adam. I'll come back after I have done my shopping to see if there is further news. Meanwhile, I will do as you suggest and pray.'

For a long time after Jess had left Adam Bond lay in the darkness behind his bandages, somehow comforted by her visit. He had never once imagined that Tamily might be his wife; maybe in dreams he had thought how wonderful it would be. But he was far too much of a realist ever to believe that such dreams could materialize. Even if she had not been in love with her husband, there was the fact of his approaching blindness—he had thought a certainty—that put marriage to any woman beyond his reach. It would be had enough being dependent upon strangers—but to be a burden to a woman he loved would be more than he could have borne.

Now, as if by way of compensation, God had provided him with a new hope. He had asked Jess to pray for him and he himself was praying, too. If one believed at all in some godlike Fate, then it would seem that the accident on the farm that had brought him to this very hospital was specially designed so that a cure might be found before it was too late. Perhaps it had also been ordained that Dick Allenton should have arrived at the precise moment to save his life.

No, he was very far from despair. While there was hope, there was much to live and be grateful for, even though there was no hope at all of his ever marrying the woman he loved. Now at least there was a chance that he might keep his job; stay near Tamily and her family and be her friend. She had already told him he could be godfather to her baby. He would become part of their family—on the outskirts perhaps, but still part of and close to those he loved. He would not be entirely alone.

He settled back quietly on his pillows and lost himself in prayer.

Tamily lay in the high sterile hospital bed, her face pale but strangely serene. Despite everything that had happened she was happy. She had not, after all, lost her baby. That in itself was wonderful news. Enough to make her eager to get well and strong again.

Over by the window, Dick was fast asleep in the only comfortable chair in the room. Her eyes wandered from the fair curly head to the long lashes on his cheeks. He looked so very young—almost like the schoolboy Dick. In a way he hadn't really changed much since those days. He was still mischievous but his mischief was now adult and therefore more harmful. At the same time he was not and never had been intentionally cruel—just thoughtless.

With a strange new maturity, Tamily doubted whether all the promises he had made an hour ago would ever be kept. He'd sworn eternal faithfulness; life-long unselfish devotion; a ceaseless concern for her and the children! No, Dick could never change overnight into a paragon of virtues—not her Dick. But although she certainly did not want a repetition of the Carol affair, she was no longer sure she *wanted* him changed. Certainly not too greatly changed. In a way, his very attraction lay in his boyish wayward enthusiasms, his sudden wild impulses and thoughtless headstrong flinging of his whole self into the new idea of the moment. For him to become predictable, steady, reliable was to change the very essence of the man she had married.

'This is real love!' she thought a trifle sadly. 'This loving not in spite of his faults *but because of them*. I love him as he is.'

She felt as if a door had been opened for her into a new understanding. With this new awareness, she allowed her thoughts to carry her on still further—to Adam Bond. In a way, she loved him, too, and loved in him those things which were missing in Dick. Perhaps, had there never been a Dick in her life, she could have married Adam and been quite happy. But not, she knew, with this same degree of intensity. Her life with Dick must be lived on the crest or the trough of a wave. Never on a calm kind current on which she could drift. It might have been like that with Adam who was gentle and kind and full of tenderness.

Dick would probably never understand how near he had come to losing her to Adam. For a little while she had lain in this bed hating Dick, wishing she need never see him again; wishing the divorce were already over and that she was free to go to Adam; to receive his love and his care.

She had thought a great deal about Adam's approaching blindness; had questioned whether she was strong enough to help him when the time came. She had known then that part of her deep affection for him was borne of pity. She had told herself that this was not necessarily wrong. Love, no matter whence the source, must be a good and beneficial thing.

Then, suddenly, Fate had brought an end to such dreams. Fate had decided Adam should have his first bad attack in the middle of that terrible bull-pen; that Dick should have been there and, with total disregard for his own safety, jumped in to save Adam's life.

Remembering it now, she could almost smile about it. It was so typical of Dick to show thoughtless, reckless courage and equally typical of him to admit afterwards that he simply hadn't stopped to consider the danger.

'So don't call me a hero!' he'd said. 'Because much as I'd like to go up a few steps in your estimation, I wasn't being brave. I never noticed the danger until I was committed!'

She had meant only to thank him; had agreed to see him just for that one purpose—to thank him for saving Adam's life. But those few minutes had been enough to show her how much she still loved him. Maybe he had read her thoughts in her eyes. Maybe it was just that the moment was tense with emotion; but when he had dropped on his knees beside the bed and whispered:

'Tam, darling, I love you so much! Can't you please forgive me?' she had known that she could never leave him.

They had talked for an hour undisturbed. Dick had made all his explanations and excuses; Tamily had tried to explain about Adam. They'd talked about the baby and the future and had held hands like an engaged couple. Then the nurse came in with Tamily's tea and it was she who noticed the fatigue in Dick's face.

'You look as if you could do with a good sleep, Mr Allenton!' she said shrewdly.

'I don't want to go home—I want to

stay here with my wife!' Dick had argued like a small boy.

'Well, have a snooze over there by the window!' the girl said. 'I don't suppose anyone will mind. It's lucky you have a private room, Mrs Allenton.'

So Dick slept and Tamily rested, watching him and thinking about the past and the future. She was thinking about Adam when the same nurse tiptoed into the room and handed her a note.

'From your mother!' she whispered. 'She said you'd want to know the news right away but she wouldn't come in when I told her you already had a visitor.'

The note was all that Tamily needed to make life perfect once more. Jess had written:

I've just come back from a visit to Adam. The leg is healing beautifully but that is only part of the good news. He had a visit yesterday evening from an American eye specialist who was on holiday from New York and calling on a colleague in the hospital. It seems that a new cure has been found for people with injuries like Adam's. It hasn't been accepted as a cure yet in this country and only a few people in America have so

*far had the operation. However, there is now
every chance that Adam can regain his sight.
All that is needed is for the fare to be found
for him to fly to the States as soon as his leg
is better.*

*Lord Allenton will pay his fare and expenses,
I know, so the future looks brighter for Adam
than it has done for months. I hope it is looking
brighter for you, too, darling.*

Your loving Mother

Tamily held the letter tightly in her
hands. When Dick woke she would show
it to him. She knew him so well, she could
predict what he would say.

'If Dad won't cough up we'll give Bond
our farm savings, won't we, Tam?'

He wouldn't stop to ask her if that's
what *she* wanted; if she thought it was
best for both of them and for Mercia
and the coming baby. He'd give Adam
their last penny with the same impulsive
enthusiasm as he would gamble it away.
That was Dick—heedless but generous;
thoughtless but kind. A strange mixture,
but nevertheless the man she had married,
the man she loved. She would never doubt
her own heart again.

This Large Print Book for the Partially sighted, who cannot read normal print, is published under the auspices of

THE ULVERSCROFT FOUNDATION

THE ULVERSCROFT FOUNDATION

. . . we hope that you have enjoyed this Large Print Book. Please think for a moment about those people who have worse eyesight problems than you . . . and are unable to even read or enjoy Large Print, without great difficulty.

You can help them by sending a donation, large or small to:

**The Ulverscroft Foundation,
1, The Green, Bradgate Road,
Anstey, Leicestershire, LE7 7FU,
England.**
or request a copy of our brochure for more details.

The Foundation will use all your help to assist those people who are handicapped by various sight problems and need special attention.

Thank you very much for your help.